To the team at the Reading Agency, who do such brilliant work
—A.M.

To Thomas "Giraffles" Jefferson, Beth Goodyear, and all my friends at SBT
—P.E.

Text copyright © 2019 by Andy McNab and Phil Earle
Illustrations copyright © 2019 by Robin Boyden

The rights of Andy McNab, Phil Earle, and Robin Boyden to be identified as the authors and illustrator of this work have been asserted by them.

Library of Congress Cataloging-in-Publication Data available

ISBN 978-1-338-61503-6

10 9 8 7 6 5 4 3 2 1   20 21 22 23 24

Printed in the U.S.A.   40
This edition first printing 2020

Book design by Stephanie Yang

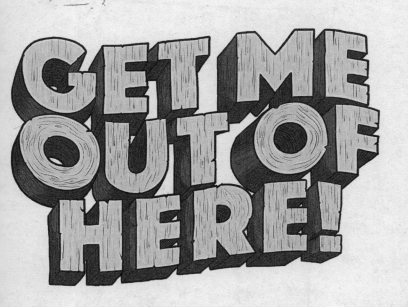

GET ME OUT OF HERE!

ANDY McNAB   PHIL EARLE

ILLUSTRATED BY ROBIN BOYDEN

Scholastic Inc.

GORGE AND
ROPE BRIDGE

ZIP LINE

"Easy," I tell myself. "Simple. Piece of cake."

Then . . . I don't move.

Minutes pass. So many that I start to feel sick from nerves.

"Don't be a wimp," I say out loud. "You've seen plenty of others do it."

I have as well, kids older and younger, plus I've jumped waaay farther myself. Only thing is, those jumps were at ground level, and this isn't.

All right, I'm standing on a brick wall that's only my height, but right now it feels like I'm balancing on top of an electrical tower that also happens to be at the highest point of Mount Everest.

So here I am, heart sweating, forehead pounding—it might be the other way around, but I don't know anymore. All I know is these two things:

A. I'm not getting down until I jump the gap to the opposite wall.

And . . .

B. I no longer WANT to jump the gap to the opposite wall.

I should've brought a hat, coat, sleeping bag, and pillow up here with me, because by the time I finally do jump it's going to be dark . . . and cold.

I look down at my shoes, high-tops with built-in swoosh, made to be springy. The sort of shoes you slam-dunk in.

The only trouble is, my feet aren't the first ones to wear them. At least one other pair lived in them before Mom found them in the thrift shop, and now they feel more like concrete-filled boots than Nike Airs.

The glue holding the soles to the leather probably weighs a few pounds alone, and as much as I love them (secondhand or not) I reckon it'll be these shoes that will see me fall to my death (or at least graze my knee), not the fact that I'm a clumsy, short-legged chicken.

My brain does this for ages, whirring and clunking until I'm pulled back to reality by a gentle tap on the shoulder that nearly shocks me off the wall and into the void.

"You jumping or not?" a voice asks.

A voice that belongs to a boy two years below me at school. "'Cause if you want, we could go first." He points to another four kids behind him, one of them even younger than he is.

I feel my cheeks flush, like I've been blowing up balloons nonstop since the day I was born. I want to ask them why they aren't in bed yet, or in front of the

TV in their pajamas. I don't say anything though. Just wave them through, like I'm doing them a favor by letting them get their jumps in before their moms call them in.

One by one they jump. All of them make it. One even does it with a spin and I instantly hate him, but also want to be him. Even though he's only eight.

And I have to do it now, don't I. Especially since they're all standing there watching, with big beaming grins on their faces.

I close my eyes and breathe in, then feel a bit dizzy.

Come on, Danny, I tell myself. Then the boys tell me the same.

I open my eyes—it'd be ridiculous to jump with them closed—then count to three in my head, launching off my right foot before I change my mind.

Wind rushes past me, and I'm in the air for what seems like ages. I'm going to crush it—probably fly right over the boys themselves. I even get ready to salute as I pass them.

But then something weird happens.

The air turns to pudding, and my legs turn to lead. I start falling instead of soaring, and I grasp at the air as if I'm trying to find an invisible ladder that quite clearly isn't there.

The wall's close, but not close enough and, most importantly, my feet are miles from it. No way are they going to land on top. My fingertips do though, biting into the bricks, giving me just enough of a grip to hang on. The rest of me slams into the wall, but I don't feel it. There's not enough room in my brain to know whether I've hurt myself or not.

I can't let go—I'd look like the biggest loser ever. One of the kids even tells me so. Another one offers me a hand but I ignore it, pulling myself up with every bit of strength I have.

It feels like it takes me ages. Like someone could build a wall quicker than I could climb this one, but, eventually, with a grunt so loud it belongs in a zoo, I pull myself onto the top, every bit of me sweating.

It's then that I feel my left leg stinging, then

the other one, then my left elbow, then the other one—well, you get the message. Within seconds, my entire body feels like one gigantic bruise, but it's nothing compared to my wounded pride. Feels like I'd need a million stitches to fix that, especially because the boys are standing over me, pointing and grinning. I notice that most of them have lost their front teeth, which is lucky for them, because I'd happily punch them all out otherwise. Well, maybe if my hands weren't stinging so much.

"Want me to call your mom for you?" one of them asks. I can't tell if he's teasing me or not.

"No thanks," I say, my voice a lot higher than it was two minutes ago, and I pull myself to my feet.

"Where you going now?"

I didn't even know until he asked me, but now I do know—instantly.

"Back there," I say, pointing at the other wall. "I'm not going in until I land on my feet." And with a hobble and limp, I make my way back.

The boys don't laugh or giggle or point, but they don't stay to watch either. They just shuffle off, one of them saying, "Gotta hand it to him," as he goes, which makes me smile and feel a little bit bigger and in less pain than I am.

I *will* make the jump. Even if it takes all day.

Just you watch me.

The day starts like all the others, just as I like it.

I don't need an alarm because the sun wakes me up, beaming through the space where the curtains should be hanging, but instead they're lying on the floor, curtain rod still attached. It's like they only fell down yesterday, when actually it was weeks ago.

I tried to put them back up loads of times, honest, but my bedroom wall has more holes in it than the surface of the moon, and in the end I gave up.

Anyway, it means I can soak in the view

twenty-four seven. Living on the seventeenth floor is incredible. The skyline's epic, and I can pretty much see everything that's going on out there without anyone being able to see me, which makes me feel like James Bond on surveillance . . . except I don't quite have his gadgets, just a penknife with a missing toothpick and blunt scissors. Still, I like it up here.

Breakfast goes the same way as always too, which means trying to duck underneath Dylan as he does pull-ups in the kitchen doorway.

"Fifty-seven . . . fifty eight," he grunts, though I know there's no way he's done that many. To be honest, I am sort of impressed. I had no idea he could count that high.

"Trying to count your brain cells again?" I ask, but regret it immediately when he wraps his legs around my neck and squeezes like a famished python.

"Don't mess with the best," he hisses, "'cause the best don't mess."

It's a line I've heard pretty much every day of my life, and I'm not concerned when the blood pumping in my ears blocks most of it out. I think he heard it in some army movie years ago, so he rolls it out whenever he can. He even went through a phase of sketching it on his arm like a fake tattoo, but didn't like it when I volunteered to draw it on his forehead instead for maximum effect. I got an extra-tight squeeze that morning, I can tell you.

As per usual, there's only one person who can release me from D.'s death grip, and that's Mom.

"Dylan, put your little brother down, please," she sighs without looking up from her phone. She must be able to hear me choking from the other side of the room. Ears like a bat, she has. She doesn't look up when I sit next to her either, gasping and rubbing at my poor strangled neck. I don't get upset that she's distracted though. It's not like she's on Facebook or anything; she's looking at the same thing she's always looking at, her banking app, frowning as she does it.

My mom works like a horse. More jobs than Dylan can count up to, that's for sure. Most mornings I don't get to see her before school,

because she's long gone. First, cleaning down at the hospital before trekking across town to the big offices, where she scrubs up after even more people. She must be amazing at vacuuming, the amount of it she does. I just wish she could vacuum up a few of the red numbers that are flashing on her screen. It might make her look a bit less stressed.

"Everything okay, Mom?" I ask.

"Living the dream, love," she replies, though from the bags under her eyes, it looks like the dream is full of rats, vampires, and clogged toilets instead of unicorns, rainbows, and five-star living.

"Nice one," I say, before asking for lunch money, which she plucks, coin by coin by coin, from her purse. By the time she's finished my pockets are going to weigh a ton, and I make a note not to walk by the canal. If I fall in, that'll be it: death by small change.

"All right, I'm off," she says, kissing my forehead but not even thinking about doing the same to Dylan, who's putting on the most elaborate floor exercises ever witnessed outside of a break dancing class. "No joining the army before I get home, Dyl, you hear?"

"I wish," he grunts with a far-off look in his eye. "Anything to get away from this loser."

"Play nicely with your brother . . ."

"Or else?"

"You'll have me to deal with." She smiles. "And remember, don't mess with the best . . ."

I stifle a laugh, loving the fact that maybe it's not just me—maybe she knows just how big of a loser he is too. But before I can ask her, she tucks her umbrella under her arm like it's a rifle and marches out the door, leaving me to follow behind.

I don't want to hang around (the last thing I need is to be used as Dylan's punching bag), so I decide to leave with my nose still intact.

8:23 a.m.

Time for school.

And Giraffles will be waiting for me downstairs.

15

3

That wasn't a spelling mistake, by the way. I know you think it should say "giraffe," like the animal, but "Giraffles" is actually spot-on.

Thomas Jefferson Raffles, to give him his full, presidential name, though no one calls him that, not even his parents or teachers. Because, by some brilliant coincidence, Tommy was born with a really, REALLY long neck, leaving him with only one possible nickname: GIRAFFLES.

Don't bother to try and make up any other jokes

about him either, because they've already been made:

YES, he always beats the lunch line by craning his neck to the front.

NO, he never loses a race, because he always wins by a neck.

YES, he can cheat on any test. It's easier to cheat when you can see everyone's answers.

But the best thing about Giraffles is that he's my best friend and he'll always stick his neck out for me if I need him.

I find him in the usual place, waiting by the elevator on the ground floor of my apartment complex, gazing dreamily into the distance.

"What's up, G.?" I say. "What you looking at? Juicy leaves at the top of that tree?"

"Yes, bro. Though I wish it was a slice of toast. Woody ate all the breakfast before I even got up."

I nod, feeling his pain. Big brothers are cretins, no matter whose roof they live under.

"You limping?" he asks.

18

I hadn't noticed before, but my knee is still sore, and not just because the elevator had broken down again.

"Little bit," I say.

"Battle wound from dissing Dylan?"

"Nah, banged my knee up on the wall over there."

"You're not still dreaming of being a free runner, are you?"

"Well, there's nothing else to do around here, is there? I haven't gotten anywhere near the Xbox in months since Dyl saved up for the new *Call of Duty*, and I'm not very good at sports, am I."

"But . . . *free running*? You have to be crazy to do that. Call me boring, but I can't see the fun in backflipping off the top of a garage. And anyway, aren't you a bit small for it? The guys who are good at it are all built like spaghetti and you're more of a baked bean. No offense."

He has a point, but I'm not going to let him get away with it.

"Maybe you should climb the wall with me. Then I can use your neck as a bridge."

"Hilarious," he says, though his face says otherwise. He's heard every insult before, after all.

We rest the banter for a while and settle on a bit of complaining instead: teachers, brothers, homework; there's nothing we can't gripe about if we put our minds to it, though to be honest, I haven't got much to complain about, other than being too young to play the lottery. A new pair of high-tops with built-in bounce won't buy themselves . . .

It's not long before the school crowd builds up around us. Marcus and Maureen tag along as always, finishing each other's sentences and reading each other's minds as only twins can.

"Are you limping?" Marcus asks me.

"'Course he is," Maureen answers for me.

"Dylan dead-leg you again?" he asks.

"Not this time," Maureen says, making me wonder if she can read my mind too. Though I certainly hope not, because she's freaking me out right now.

"He's been falling off walls again, haven't you, Danny?"

I nod. No point lying about it, especially if she really is inside my brain.

Their names do make me laugh though: MandM, you know, like the candy. And what makes it worse is that their mom and

dad are called Mike and Molly. You couldn't make it up, could you? They must've had the worst baby name book to choose from.

Anyway, I try to shut them up about my limp by running at every wall I can see, to show them

I have got skills, but, to be honest, they don't look very interested.

Giraffles' head is in the clouds, almost literally, while MandM are talking in some sort of twin code that could be either highly sophisticated or complete gobbledygook.

Either way, it leaves me to focus on the dream of being the best free runner in the country. And by the time we reach the school gates, I'm smashing it left, right, and center, front-flipping off mailboxes and swan diving off walls, leaving the lanky spaghetti kids trailing in my dust.

Too bad the bell has to go and ring, right at my most triumphant moment. I sigh heavily and file into class. Reality sometimes really does suck.

4

"School" isn't a dirty word.

"Puddle" *kind of* is.

"Mud" *definitely* is.

But "school"?

Not so much.

Others disagree. They complain about it nonstop, and that's all right: I don't have to listen or anything. I don't have to agree either.

OK, there are bits of it that suck. Whoever invented fractions was a bit weird, and don't get me started on the idiot who came up with conjunctive adverbs (I mean, what even are they anyway?), but there's loads of stuff about school that's all right, really.

PE, for starters, and history, and that magic twenty minutes every day when we drop everything and get read to. Who doesn't like laying their head on their desk while someone tells them a story? Weirdos, that's who.

Anyway, school's all right with me. And it's particularly all right this year because we lucked out and got Miss D. as our teacher. The teacher every class wanted and only we got. Cue much flossing to celebrate.

Miss D. is the best, in every way.

It's like being taught by someone who is one part mom, one part cool aunt, one part friend, and one part encyclopedia.

She isn't tall. She's real short, which is maybe a big part of why I like her, but she's not a pushover. No way. She's strict when she needs to be, a real firecracker, but she just makes everything . . . fun.

Well, almost everything. She makes conjunctive adverbs bearable, which is a feat in itself.

"Hiya, Danny, manage to avoid Dylan this morning?" She smiles as we file in, finding something different to say to every one of us, whether it's about new shoes or what we watched on TV last night.

It makes me smile and feel good as I take my seat next to Lucky.

Lucky Success.

Never has a name suited anyone more. Honestly, it's like he has the Midas touch. Everything he touches doesn't just turn to gold, it's like the gold is encrusted with jewels too. And I mean, *everything*.

I swear that boy sneezes diamonds and farts unicorns.

He's the most talented athlete in school, the best at math, and has a lighthouse smile that my mom says could charm the birds from the trees.

Lucky lives in the biggest house, with his own room and Xbox, plus his sister is super cute (tell anyone I said that and I'll put you in one of Dyl's chokeholds). He doesn't milk being the best at so many things, or lord it over you. If he's got a bag of candy he'll share some with you; if he's got a new game on his new phone he's happy to let you have a turn. And that makes him all right by me.

Plus he's smart, and he never covers up his answers in a test, which makes him doubly OK. He's a bit too perfect to ever replace old Giraffles, but as a desk buddy I could do a lot worse.

"You get the new battle passes for *Fortnite*?" he asks as I sit down.

"Oh yeah . . ." I reply, though I had no idea there were any new ones. I gave up online gaming months ago. Broadband doesn't exist in our apartment building. Somewhere in the basement there's probably a hamster in a wheel breaking a mean sweat, but no matter how hard he spins he's never going to make our internet fast enough.

"We should play online together." He grins.

"Too much free running to do."

"Yeah, I could see you were still doing that from your limp on the way in."

I feel my cheeks flush as my brain searches for a speedy comeback. Fortunately, Miss D. interrupts with the roll call before breaking into what she calls an "Exciting Opportunity."

"As you know, the end of the semester is fast approaching . . ."

Cue cheers from the back row.

". . . I know, I know, we're all excited about the Easter holiday. But before we have a well-earned break from adjectives and long division, something a bit special has come up."

"Have we all won the lottery?" shout MandM

27

at exactly the same time, sending a shiver of freakiness up my spine.

"I don't think any of us would still be sitting here if that was the case," beams Miss D.

"Oh no, we're not being visited by the president, are we?" asks Giraffles, a question so random it makes me wonder if his long neck has somehow starved his brain of oxygen.

"Hardly, Thomas. I certainly wouldn't be smiling if we were. No, we've been invited on a very special trip . . ."

Cue groans from the back.

"Please tell me we don't have to go to the water treatment plant again, Miss D."

"Or to the history museum. Piles of old bones are so boring . . ."

I've got to be honest, I'm not exactly jumping out of my seat either. I think it's some sort of ancient law that school trips have to be:

A. Absolutely garbage

B. Absolutely boring

C. ABSOLUTELY predictable.

I know where we're going: Tickledown Farm. The sixth-grade class goes there *every year*. Dyl went before he left for junior high. The trip leader makes the oldest kids go with the youngest to "build empathy." But Dyl reckons it's just so the teachers can put their feet up and drink coffee all day.

I'm not so sure. Can't imagine Miss D. would be up for that either. She looked just as grossed out by the smell of the sewage plant as we did.

"I can see you're all incredibly excited by the news. So instead of letting me bore you with the details . . . why don't you just watch this?"

With a flick of her wrist and a tap on the whiteboard, a film begins. And the second it starts, I feel my pulse race and my palms sweat.

I feel a rush of adrenaline hit me, like I'm standing on top of the most colossal wall in the world, because on the screen are six beautiful, exciting, eye-popping words:

ARE YOU READY . . . TO GO WILD?

"IMAGINE A PLACE . . ." the voice-over purrs, **"WHERE YOU CAN LIVE OUT YOUR WILDEST DREAMS . . ."**

I'm already in. I've signed on the dotted line, I've packed my bag, and kissed Mom goodbye. What comes next only makes me even more excited.

"Where you can climb the steepest mountains, before jumping from the top . . ."

I wipe away a bit of spit that's escaped from the corner of my gaping mouth. I can't believe what I'm seeing. The biggest rock face I've ever laid eyes on, so high the top of it disappears into the sky, which is so blue I swear it's been airbrushed by a Smurf.

And there, stuck to the side of the rock, is a kid just like me, except with a helmet and ropes attached to him. He's smiling like a loon, just like I am now. And though it looks like hard work, it also looks like the best work ever. And there isn't a conjunctive whatchamacallit anywhere to be seen.

The film goes on. And it just gets better, because there are kayaks and rapids, zip lines and tree houses, and the entire time there's this voice, like the one you hear in a *Star Wars* trailer, telling me: **"BREATHE DEEP, FASTEN YOUR SAFETY BELT, AND PREPARE TO GO WILD AT WILD OUT!"**

The film ends with a kid zooming down a zip line at a hundred miles an hour, and when the screen goes black, there's a huge cheer from the classroom, and applause and whooping.

And then I realize that all that noise is coming

from me. And that everyone is looking at me, and laughing and pointing, but I don't care because I've just seen the greatest thing in the world ever, better than jumping off any wall, better than a hundred walls that are taller than the Empire State Building. And even though I don't know when we're going to Wild Out, I'm already counting down the days in my head until we get on the bus.

"You're excited, then, Danny?" asks Miss D., with a smile almost as big as mine.

In my head I'm going to reply with a shrug and a nod and a "yeah-it-looks-OK" . . . but what actually happens is that

I throw both hands in the air and shout, as loud as voice-over man himself, **"MISS D., I AM ALL OVER IT!"**

Cue more laughter and pointing.

Trips to the water treatment plant are a thing of the past! This is the future, and the future is so flipping bright I might need a pair of sunglasses just so I don't get a headache from all the excitement.

"I'm pleased you're so pleased," Miss D. continues. "It really is a wonderful opportunity for us. To visit a place where the landscape is so different from everything we're used to. Make no mistake, it will be challenging, like nothing any of us have ever experienced . . ."

"Come on, Miss D.," laughs Lucky beside me. "We've grown up in the city. It's a jungle *here*. There's nothing in the outdoors that's going to scare us. It's not like we're going to get mugged by a sheep, are we?"

Others agree. Marcus and Maureen shout,

"Yeah!" at exactly the same time, while Giraffles looks properly excited as well. Probably because he's thinking about all the leaves at the top of those tall, tall trees.

"Well, we'll see, won't we," adds Miss D., though her face suggests she knows something that none of us do. "All you have to do, to secure a spot on the trip, is return this letter by next week, signed by your parents or guardians."

And she passes around the note. I try to read it, but fail. All I can see are the words "WILD OUT," which makes me so unbelievably excited that I fear I might actually combust. The rest of the words are swimming in a million different directions, and, anyway, the details aren't important.

All that matters is that I'm going to be on that bus. I'm going to climb everything they put in front of me. I am literally going to be the WILDEST kid they have ever met.

And then I read the sentence that brings me crashing back down to earth.

"Whoa. A hundred and fifty bucks?"

Oh.

Of course.

We have to *pay* to go.

My eyes scour the letter, and suddenly the words "WILD OUT" seem like the smallest ones on the page. The only words I can see, and I can still see them even when I close my eyes in fear and disappointment, are:

Dear Parent or Guardian,

The cost of this once-in-a-lifetime opportunity is $150. While we understand it is a considerable sum of money, we are confident it is a trip that none of our students will forget.

Sincerely,

I open my eyes, but the words are still there and I can't erase them, not with a pencil, not with a flipping nuclear bomb.

I look around me. Lucky doesn't look worried, but then his dad works in one of those huge offices in the city, doesn't he?

Giraffles isn't sweating either, and neither are MandM, though they are blowing their noses at the same time and making exactly the same noise.

The only person who looks even vaguely disturbed by this gargantuan bombshell is me.

One hundred and fifty bucks.

I headbutt the desk in despair.

Going wild?

I won't be going anywhere.

"You wouldn't last two minutes in the wild anyway," laughs Dyl above the whirring of his hair clippers.

It's one of his most annoying habits (one of many, many, many), shaving his own head in the kitchen. I wouldn't mind if he did it over a piece of newspaper, but he never does. Today he's simply leaning over the table, showering the fruit bowl with his greasy stubble. I swear he only buzzes his head like this because he's too lazy to wash it.

I cringe, forcing the image of eating a hairy apple clear out of my mind.

Fortunately for Dylan, Mom's paying him no attention: She's still poring over the letter from school, with a huge frown on her face. Normally, she saves that look for when she's reading my idiot brother's report card, but today I know it's me causing her grief.

I did think about not showing it to her. I could have crumpled it into a ball and chucked it in the trash on my way home. At least that way I wouldn't keep torturing myself by reading and rereading about a trip I'll never get to go on.

But for some reason, I didn't; I just handed it over sheepishly, with a "Sorry, Mom."

She hasn't said anything since; she just sighs repeatedly and alternates between reading the letter, sighing some more, and peering at the bank app on her phone, presumably in the hope that she can magically make a hundred and fifty dollars appear out of thin air.

In the end, she finally says what I already know.

"I'm really sorry, Dan, but I just can't afford it.

Dylan's got boot camp coming up, plus he's grown about a foot in the last six weeks, so he needed a whole new uniform on top of everything else." Dyl kisses his bicep and gazes at it adoringly like it's Ariana Grande or something.

"I'll pay you back, Mom . . ." I say, feeling guilty as I say it.

"It's not about that, love. I don't doubt that for even a minute. I just don't have it to give to you."

"What if I sold some stuff to pay for it? Old clothes, maybe."

There's a laugh behind me. "NO ONE wants to buy your dirty old shorts."

"I'd sell you if I thought anyone would give me five bucks, but I'd probably have to pay *them* to take you away."

I feel Dyl's response before I hear it: a fist to the back, which really hurts, though I refuse to even flinch. His ego doesn't need any inflating; it's already the size of a hot-air balloon.

"Do you think school would let me pay them back,

41

then? You know, before the end of the semester?"

"I doubt it. They're always begging us for donations, so the chances of them paying your way are as small as—"

"Danny's six-pack?" adds Dyl, unhelpfully.

What he doesn't realize, though, is that every time he opens his mouth, I become more determined. I want to show him I'm every bit as outdoorsy and up for it as he is. That he's not the only one who can climb a rope or save a hostage from behind enemy lines.

It's like Mom is reading my mind too, because from nowhere she pipes up with a lifeline. A twenty-four-karat-gold lifeline.

"Fifty dollars," she says.

"What is?" I reply.

"That's what I can give you. For now. If you can raise the rest, then you can go, Dan. I'd love to lend it all to you, you know I would, but unless we give up eating for the next four weeks, that's the best I can do."

I do the math—one hundred dollars.

That's what I have to raise.

In a week.

"One hundred dollars," I say out loud, which provokes another scoff from behind me.

"No chance," laughs Dyl. "You couldn't raise a hundred pennies." I glare at him while he goes back to shaving his oversized head.

And it's at that exact moment that I know, surer than ever, that I'm going to raise that money. And that my idiot brother, without even realizing, or lifting a finger, is going to help me.

"Are you sure about this, D.?" asks Giraffles, squirming on the stool.

"Of course I am, bro," I reply. "If Dylan can cut his own hair with these, then I'm sure I can cut someone else's with them."

"Maybe you should start with your own mop though? Looks like it could do with a trim."

I ignore the insult and focus on where to start. The clippers are still recharging, so the most difficult part is making the cord stretch to the top of Giraffles' telescopic neck. I momentarily consider an extension cord, or two even, joined together.

"What style are you after, then, sir?" I ask, practicing my best customer service.

"None. I'm growing it out." Giraffles tries to stand up and leave, but I push him down with my firm grip.

"You know what'd suit you? A slick David Beckham cut. All shaved and sharp edges."

"Mmmmm . . ." He doesn't sound convinced, but he doesn't say no either, so I take that as my cue to start, the clippers already vibrating in my slightly shaking hands.

And do you know what? It goes all right. I manage to not chop off his head, and I don't think he even notices when I catch the top of his ear and make it bleed a tiny bit.

The curls fall to the ground, and with every strand I feel my confidence grow. I even start making chitchat, asking my customer if he's got plans for the weekend or if he's been on vacation lately. I get nothing back, though, and I can see

Giraffles' knuckles turning white as he grips the leg of the stool.

Twelve brisk minutes later, I'm done, and after whipping off the dish towel like a matador's cape, I confidently hand Giraffles a mirror.

He says nothing, though his face does change color. A lot. First it's green, then it goes deathly gray, and as his eyes burn into the mirror a lot of red starts to appear.

"What have you done?" he yells. "David Beckham does NOT have his hair cut like this!"

"He would if he came here," I reply defensively. "It's the only style I can do. Besides, now that you're bald I've just saved you ten minutes in the morning, PLUS you won't have to buy any gel for a good two months."

"I hate it."

"It'll grow back, bro."

"Yeah, maybe, but what about the top of my ear? Maybe we can find that on the floor and glue it back on."

47

Giraffles sulks, with his arms crossed and everything, for a good fourteen-and-a-half minutes before I shove a plate of cookies in front of him and allow him to graze calmly.

"You're not really going to charge people for this torture, are you?" he says eventually.

"'Course I am. Buzz cuts are very in at the moment, and most kids pay like ten bucks down at the barber."

"But how will people know to come here to get it done? You live closer to the moon than you do the ground."

"Aha, well these little beauties are rechargeable, aren't they, so I'm going to set up my own pop-up shop around the corner from Jack's Barbers. Battery life is two hours and it'll take me fifteen minutes per haircut, so that's enough for eight customers before I have to recharge. If people pay me four bucks a haircut, that's thirty-two dollars before I even have to plug it back in. I'll have the cash in no time!"

Giraffles doesn't look so sure, and asks to

borrow the thickest beanie I own despite it being the middle of April.

But, a mere thirty minutes later, we're all set up with a kitchen stool, a dish towel, a mirror, and a tub of Dylan's gel (so at least it *looks* like I can do more than one style).

I've even painted a sign on an old box, saying:

"Spelling error," barks Giraffles.

"It's *cool*," I reply.

"You're an idiot. I bet you won't make it fifteen minutes before you're using that towel to stop your own nose from bleeding . . ."

But I haven't got time for worrying. This is going to work. It's got to.

At first, it does! 'Cause I work out who to target.

Kids younger and smaller than me, that's the

key. Kids who can't physically hurt me when I buzz them; kids who have a ten-dollar bill in their pocket from their mom for a trim, and are delighted when I tell them they can keep some of it to spend on candy.

One by one they perch on the stool, and they don't so much as flinch as I shear them, not even when I get a bit careless with the clippers. Some of them are even happy with what I've done. One kid, who to be fair to him did wear the thickest glasses known to man, even gave me a tip.

After no time at all I have twenty-nine dollars nestling in my pocket. If I'd known it was going to be this easy, I'd have set up my business months ago.

But then, there's a glitch. Well, I say a glitch; it's more a gut-emptying horror show of a catastrophe, for as my back is turned, to professionally and expertly blow the stray hairs off my clippers, I get a new, unexpected customer, who is neither younger nor smaller than me. In fact, he's bigger than most adults. He's so big, he makes Giraffles look like Thumbelina.

Tubs Wilkinson has taken up residence on the stool, and he's already tied the towel around his tree-trunk neck.

Tubs isn't tubby. At all. *He's ripped*. All over. He's the only teenager on the planet who has a six-pack on his forehead.

He's not a *complete* tank. Not quite. Though lifting weights twenty-three hours a day does seem to have done something to the way his brain works . . . and he is known for random acts of extreme violence. Though, happily, never at me . . . until now.

"Take it all off," he grunts by way of a welcome.

"R-r-really?" I stammer. "But you've been growing your hair for ages."

He has. It reaches his shoulders and there's loads of it. In fact, his hair looks just like the rest of him: muscular. You could probably knit a rope bridge out of his super-strength locks, I think as I stare at them.

"All of it. And do it quick. I'm due down at the gym in twenty minutes. Do NOT make me late."

I have no idea what to do next.

Do I do it, mess it up, and potentially live the rest of my life as a human bruise?

Or do I suddenly develop a chronic wrist injury that ends my promising career as barber to the stars . . .

"Come on, I'm waiting," he grunts.

So I start up the clippers, step forward, and gulp, even though the tennis ball in my throat refuses to budge . . .

I am exactly three seconds into the haircut when I realize I am in serious trouble.

Tubs' hair is way too long and lustrous for the clippers to make even the smallest of dents in it.

In fact, it's worse than that, as the hair simply gets locked in the machine's teeth, which grind and howl before yanking his head back like I've pulled it.

"Noooooooooooo," I howl under my breath, but fortunately Tubs' neck muscles are so full-on that it feels like nothing more than a playful tug, and he keeps his eyes front and center.

"Quick," I whisper to Giraffles, who's standing wide-eyed beside me. "Hold these. Just for a minute."

He shakes his head so viciously it looks like it's in danger of rolling off his shoulders, and steps back a dozen paces. "I warned you. This was never going to end well."

But it has to. I can't mess this up without my face ending up just as mangled as Tubs' hair, if not more. So I flick the clippers off and leave them clinging to his locks, while I dive into Dylan's toiletries bag, which I stole from the bathroom cabinet.

"Come on . . ." I mouth, "there has to be some in there, has to be . . ."

I pull out Band-Aids, unused and otherwise, empty bottles of shower gel, and a deodorant that smells worse than any armpit ever did, until, with my heart screaming in panic, I find them: Dyl's nail scissors. They're small and blunt, and appear to still have one of his toenails attached to them, but they are my (and my face's) lifeline.

I return to the dangling clippers, and begin to hack around Tubs' twisted locks.

"Oh yes," I coo, acting like I know what I'm flippin' doing, "this is really starting to take shape . . ." And although it isn't, it *is* kind of working, as the clippers fall free into my hand and I continue to cut as much hair as I can from Tubs' head.

I work with speed, purely out of fear, and as the minutes go on, the hair starts to build up on top of my feet. In fact, I'm starting to look more like a hobbit than an eleven-year-old barber.

Within minutes I've cut the entire left side of his head. It's patchy, to say the least, but it's kind of all the same length.

But then, as I snip at the last strand, disaster strikes again.

The scissors—exhausted by a workout that would leave an Olympic sprinter wheezing—fall into two pieces. And no matter how hard I try, I cannot entice them back together.

In my head, I'm wailing and screaming and

panicking. Out loud I'm still cooing and bragging about how I'm creating some kind of masterpiece. Anything to not give the game away. But with every passing second I feel more and more out of control, until a little miracle pipes up in my ear.

"Buy yourself some time and use the clippers to even out the short side. I'll run and grab some more scissors from home. Mom's got a sharp pair in the kitchen."

In that moment, I could kiss old Giraffles. Well, I say that, but his neck's too long to get anywhere near his face, so I settle for a whispered thank-you, and turn the clippers back on.

The next three minutes are perfection. The clippers are working, the short hair is coming off easily, and I manage to not chop off any part of Tubs' face. It's win, win, win, and I smile as I turn my attention to the last bit of unclipped hair. Once that's done, half of the head will be complete. And I know if I can do one side, I can definitely do the other.

The clippers slide under the hair at the nape of

his neck, but then,
nothing happens.
Well, actually
that's a lie.
There's a
beep, then
another
beep, then
a third beep,
and then
nothing.
Because
the clippers
stop working
altogether.

"Is there an issue?" asks Tubs.

"No, of course not," I lie.

But there is. There really, really is. The clippers
are dead. And with a sinking feeling I remember that
the charger is back at the apartment, halfway to the
flipping moon!

I look behind me, desperate for the sight of Giraffles sprinting while simultaneously carrying a pair of super-sharp scissors.

At least if I have them I can start cutting the other half. Maybe he'd even sprint back up to the apartment and charge the clippers.

That would work. Or at least it would if he were anywhere to be seen.

"Come on," says Tubs, pouring yet more panic on top of me. "I haven't got all day."

I try to say something, but all that comes out is a jumble of terrified sounds that are barely words, never mind a sentence that makes any kind of sense.

A muscly arm shoots up in the air. "Mirror," Tubs demands.

"But . . . er . . . I'm not done yet. Only h-h-halfway through . . ."

"MIRROR." The voice is louder and full of menace and threat.

"An artist never reveals all until the masterpiece is complete!"

But Tubs is done with waiting
pulls out his phone and flicks it into
and that's it. That's all he needs to see.
he's on his feet and towering over me, one
his head as smooth as a baby's bottom, while the
other looks more like he's had an electric shock.

"What's this?" he yells, pointing at his head.

"It's not finished . . ." I reply, taking a step back.

"You bet it's not. You trying to make me look stupid?"

"'Course not. It's just my scissors. They . . ."

"They what?"

"They. Well, they . . ." I hold them up.

"You've cut my hair with *them*?"

"Er, yeah?"

"They're all rusty . . . and they're nail scissors!"

"Well, they *were*. I don't know *what* they are now, except junk maybe."

I mean it to be lighthearted. To kind of show how well I've done with garbage equipment. But all it does is infuriate him more than I thought was possible.

Before I know it, he's grabbed hold of me and flipped me upside down, holding me by the ankles and shaking me like a piggy bank.

"I want my money back!"

"But you haven't paid me yet!"

"Then I want compensation."

"For what?"

"Damages. To my reputation, and because someone has to put this mess straight."

And he carries on shaking me. Endlessly. Until my pockets give in and spit every last cent I have all over the pavement.

That's his cue to drop me and scoop up a handful of my wages. At least ten bucks' worth, I reckon.

"That should cover it," he says. "And I'd suggest you think about a different career. Come within a mile of me with a pair of scissors again and I'll rearrange your face."

And with that he departs, pulling a beanie from his pocket to hide his shame.

I feel myself deflate, but also feel relief flow over me too. Clutching my face, it feels like my nose is still where it was earlier, and so is everything else, and I have to be pleased with that.

I'm also eighteen dollars richer than I was this morning, so it's not all wrecked.

Quickly, I scamper around and scoop the money back into my pocket, only to be tapped on the shoulder by a rosy-cheeked Giraffles.

"Did you finish Tubs already?"

"Not exactly."

"I found the scissors."

"I think I'm retiring from the barber business."

"Already?"

"Yeah, not sure I'm cut out for it."

I didn't mean it to be funny, but for once Giraffles thinks I'm hilarious.

"So what are you going to do now? To pay for the trip?"

I'm about to shrug, clean out of ideas, when I see a woman walking a dog.

In fact she's not walking a dog. She's walking *eight* of them.

And my ears perk up quicker than a bloodhound's.

Bingo.

Brilliant.

I'm back in the game.

9

Ten minutes into my first ride and we're going so fast I think we might be in danger of taking off.

It is, without doubt, the most exciting husky ride of my life.

Kind of.

Because I'm not standing on a sled, I'm standing on Dyl's old scooter, and it's not being pulled by a pack of highly trained huskies, it's being dragged by nine different dogs: a dalmatian, a pit bull, a whippet, and a host of others I know nothing about other than that they are fast!

What I do know is that if they keep this up, or, rather, if their owners keep on paying me, I'll have the money in no time. In fact, I'll probably be rich enough to retire!

I grin wildly as the pack pulls me around the park. I still can't believe how easy it was to find so many customers. All I had to do was get up super early and pounce on people as they set off, bleary eyed, for their morning walk. Nobody likes scooping up dog poop at six-thirty in the morning.

Nor do they like traipsing the streets when it's pelting down with rain. Not when they could be sitting on the sofa with a steaming cup of tea and Netflix on the TV.

Which was pretty much my sales pitch, to be honest . . .

"Wouldn't you rather *I* get cold walking Bonzo instead of you? I'll pick up his poop for you this morning if you like? As many as he can squeeze out, and it'll only cost you four dollars an hour."

They bit my hand off quicker than a German shepherd that hasn't eaten in a week.

And as for the poop picking?

I haven't scooped up a single one yet. No need, because I've invented this brilliant new game called Poop Golf.

All you need to join in the fun is a stick and a poop, preferably belonging to a dog.

As soon as Fido does his business you take your stick and flick the poop into the nearest bush in as few shots as possible. You get extra points if you can flick the poop into the bush without it breaking into pieces or hitting your shoe by accident.

It's funny the games you can make up at 6:37 in the morning . . . I give it ten years before you see it in the Olympics.

Anyway, it's worked out perfectly, though it's taken me a day of having my arms pulled out of their sockets to realize that I needed a vehicle, both to exercise the dogs properly, and to give me the best rush possible.

After three hours of endless searching, I found Dyl's scooter hidden under all his army gear. And honestly, you could've lassoed Mars from Earth with the amount of rope he had stashed away. So I borrowed a bit of that too, building a harness that keeps the dogs safe while they pull me along like Usain Bolt on a superbike.

Which brings me here, beaming at joggers as I zoom past them.

And it makes me feel magical, all this speed.

Makes me hungry to get to Wild Out and beat every challenge they put in front of me.

BOULDERING? No problem, I'll make 'em look like pebbles.

RAPIDS? Pah, they don't look so quick to me . . . Right now, with the wind whipping at my face and the g-force blowing my cheeks behind my ears, I feel powerful. For the first time in forty-eight hours, the thought of being shaken upside down by Big Tubs doesn't fill me with dread and fear. Not anymore.

I feel like I could stand up to him, or Dyl, or any other meathead who comes my way.

No one can touch me. I'm Danny Mack! Prince of Speed, King of the Jungle.

Except, while I'm having these thoughts of grandeur, a cat crosses the path. And my crown most definitely slips . . .

At first, I don't think the cat is even going to move. It just stands there, eyes wide, back arched. The dogs, of course, go crazy, turning the scooter-sled into a fighter jet, but that doesn't bother the cat, which simply hisses like a teakettle, then roars like a panther, before turning on its tail and running away.

But the pack howls in reply and takes off after it, paying little attention to the rules of the road or the fact that the cat has left the path and is now racing down the gravel that leads to the skate park.

I feel the surface change under my feet, the vibrations shaking every muscle and cell in my body. I try to adapt—bend my knees, absorb as much of the track as I can—but it's tough, unforgiving, and I see my knuckles turn red, then white, as I cling to the bars of the scooter.

"WHOOOOOOOOOOOA!" I yelp, trying to remember the names of the dogs and failing miserably, but if anything, they take my plea as encouragement and hammer on even quicker, desperate to close the gap between their prey and their jaws.

The gap between the two shortens slightly, and

I do my best to steer the scooter clear of potholes and puddles. The wheels respond, somehow, and I start to feel something I don't expect: a teeny-tiny bit of control, and in return a drip-drip-drip of excitement.

I'm doing it.

I'm rolling with the punches, taking everything the dumb cat can throw at me and surfing right over the top of it.

Except then, right then, it's like the cat is listening to my thoughts and thinking, *OK, Danny Mack, let's see what you do with this*, before taking a sharp left toward the skate park.

"OH. MAAAAAAAAN." I yell, as I know only too well what is lying ahead: the most extreme array of bumps, jumps, and half-pipes imaginable. The sort of challenges that test the most able of skaters, never mind undersized idiots in charge of nine dogs and a battered scooter.

The cat is going crazy now, dashing in every direction, to avoid not only my trusty pack, but the astonished mob of skaters, who quickly start filming my every move.

They whoop as I grab some serious air off the first ramp, yell as I soar even higher off the second, then cover their eyes (but not their phones) as I head straight down into the half-pipe.

I can't begin to explain how it feels as I hit the top of the ramp and follow the dogs skyward. A little bit excited and a lotta bit scared: I think at some point I do actually let out a bit of pee in both fear and joy.

Is this how Santa Claus feels, I wonder, when Rudolph and the others pull him into the clouds?

Either way, it's not Christmas Eve, not by a long shot. And anyway, even Santa has rough landings sometimes, which is exactly what happens to me.

I've ridden my luck for as long as I can, but finally that luck gives way and the scooter flicks from under my feet, and tears at my fists, ripping them away from the handles.

Onward the dogs and the scooter fly, still in the

direction of the poor but deeply annoying cat that I swear is now laughing at me.

And as for me, I go in the only direction available: down.

Down, down, down, until a patch of grass reaches up and gives me the biggest and roughest hug of my life.

Ouch.

Ouch. Ouch. Ouch.

I wake up with an all-over body tattoo in the shape of a bruise.

It hurts and it stings—but only when I try to move any part of my body, including my eyelids.

But at the same time, I have never been so happy in my life, because on my bedside table is the biggest pile of money I have ever seen.

In my head, it looks like a million bucks, but at the same time I know that it's actually one hundred dollars. On the dot.

Most of it is coins, shining like a pile of pirate's

treasure, but there's quarters, dimes, nickels, and even one penny, which makes me really, really happy because it reminds me that I earned every single cent myself.

The pain doesn't hurt half as much, though, when you've proven a point to yourself, so I manage to have a shower and try (unsuccessfully) to tame my hair. I smile when my mom gives me a hug and hands over the final fifty dollars, though I also feel a bit guilty about taking it from her. Maybe if I'd worked a bit harder, I could've raised the whole amount myself.

I have to walk to school slowly—a result of the bruise tattoo and the fact that I'm carrying two tons of loose change in my pockets—but that only gives me more time to become even more excited about the trip.

"What are you looking forward to most?" I ask the rest of the crew.

"Bouldering," reply MandM in unison, without pause or consultation.

"Kayaking," says Giraffles, and I momentarily wonder if they'll have to make a special one to fit his epically long limbs.

Lucky takes his time before shouting the most perfect sentence imaginable:

"ALL OF IT!"

I'd jump on his back in wild agreement if my legs weren't so heavy with coins, because he's nailed it. That's EXACTLY what I'm thinking. This is going to be the most perfect trip known to man. Or woman. Or child.

And that is what I'm thinking as we walk into the schoolyard. I'm even still thinking it when I hear someone shout my name in a tone that can only be described as vicious.

"Are you Danny Mack?" It belongs to a woman with a perm as angry and wound up as her accusation.

"Er . . ." My hesitation kind of gives me away, and the woman drags a small, cowering boy out from behind her legs. A boy with a haircut so disastrous that there can only be one explanation for it. That I was his hairdresser.

"I need a word with you," she says, before continuing to shout loads of them at me. "What did you do to my Cameron? He used to have lovely hair. Like a little prince. But now? Well, thanks to you he looks like a crazed orc."

I don't know what to say, so I say the wrong thing, obviously.

"But that's the look we were going for. He told me his favorite book was *Lord of the Rings*, and let's face it, no one wants a hobbit cut. They're *so* last year."

In my head it's funny, or at least witty, but to the woman standing before me it's the final insult she's been waiting for, and just like Tubs, she threatens to turn me upside down until she gets her money back.

I save her the trouble, and me the pain and shame, by digging four bucks out of my pocket, though it isn't until I let go of the money that I realize what it means.

That I only have one hundred and forty-six dollars. And to go on the trip, I need one hundred and fifty. I feel myself sag, and my bruises start shouting a whole lot louder.

Thirty seconds later and they're screaming, when another livid mother does exactly the same thing, so I rush to the door only to be detained a third flipping time, which leads to another refund. By the time I make it to class my pockets are lighter.

Twelve bucks lighter.

And the money is due in T-minus ninety seconds. Now, I'm a quick thinker, but even I'm stumped. What can I do? Beg for more time? Beg Mom for more? I can't do either, as Miss D. made it clear that today is the absolute deadline with no exceptions.

So I slump in my seat, allowing my head to settle onto the desktop, where I intend to leave it until 3:15 p.m.

"OK, everybody, good morning," sings Miss D.

from the front. "So, who has trip money for me?"

I watch a trail of classmates wind their way to the front, fist-bumping and grinning as they sign up for the single greatest class trip ever. I push my forehead even harder onto the desktop.

"Danny?" Miss D. is calling me now. "Danny, have you got yours, dear?"

I don't know what to say. I can't say it out loud, because it's like admitting I'm a complete pauper in front of everyone I know, so, with pockets jangling, I shuffle to her desk.

"Come on, sunshine. Hand it over. I know how hard you've been working for this."

"I've decided not to go, Miss D.," I say, quietly. "Not sure it's for me." Forcing out the lie hurts way more than any bruise in the world.

Her eyes widen and her jaw goes limp. "But you've been walking all those dogs."

I feel the tears gather behind my eyes, and I know she sees it.

"What is it, Danny? You can tell me."

"I can't afford it, Miss D. I thought I could, but I can't."

She sighs, and peers over my shoulder at the rest of the class before lowering her voice as she says, "Do you have your money with you?"

I nod.

"Then pass it over and let me count it. Perhaps you've just added it up wrong."

I tell her I haven't, but she insists, so I pile the money up on her desk like a molehill, and she tells us all to get on with silent reading for ten minutes.

So we do as she says—well, the others do. I pretend to read while watching her move the money into piles, then see her frown and sigh as she too realizes that I'm twelve dollars short.

I want to look away then, out of shame, but for some reason I don't, and instead I see Miss D. reach under her desk and into her bag, where she rummages for a few seconds.

Then, with the slightest movement of hands,

she places a few bills beside my pile, before lifting her head and smiling.

"Oh, Danny, you silly boy," she grins. "We really do need to work on your addition, don't we? It's all here. A hundred and fifty dollars. Perfect."

I don't know what to say. I know what she's done, and it's just about the best and kindest thing anyone could ever do for me (except perhaps teaching me to cut hair properly). I spend the next hour until recess trying not to get all cry-y about it.

So when the bell rings and the others file out, I pretend to tie my laces, until there's only me and Miss D. left in the room.

"I know what you did," I tell her. "And I don't know what to say, except thank you."

She smiles. "I have no idea what you're talking about, Daniel Mack."

She's embarrassed now, and I don't want to make it worse. So I simply say, "I'll pay you back, Miss D. Promise I will," and walk on.

And as I reach the door, I hear her faintly reply, "I know you will, son. I know."

Off into the schoolyard I go, to find something to jump off of.

If I'm going to do this properly, then I'm going to need all the practice I can get.

There is no way I am missing the bus.

I know this because I am an hour early for it. In fact, when I arrive I'm the first person at the playground, apart from the raccoon that's rifling through the trash.

Mom gets a bit teary when I say goodbye, unlike Dyl, who doesn't even surface from his tomb of a bedroom. Mom makes up for it by pulling me into a bear hug that would surely suffocate a lesser man than me. Then the phone rings, which allows me to escape before she can do any actual damage.

I don't feel the weight of my backpack, even though it's holding just about every item of clothing I own. There were loads of things that I didn't have. I mean, who has hiking boots when they only ever set foot on city sidewalks?

And as for a headlamp: Have they never heard of streetlights? Or phones?

Anyway, the minutes pass, the excitement builds, and so does the number of us waiting in the schoolyard.

Giraffles hobbles up with a massive bag on his back that makes him look like more of a camel than a giraffe, MandM arrive in matching everything, while Lucky makes the biggest entrance. Literally everything he's wearing or carrying is brand-new and top-of-the-line, though he doesn't make a fuss about it. If anything, he looks slightly embarrassed by it all. With a bit of luck, he might have some spare stuff that I can borrow . . .

There's a cheer when the bus arrives, then a stampede as we pile on, fighting to get the seats as far away from the bathroom as possible, though we've already been warned that it's a "pee-only facility" by the driver.

Anyone attempting anything else will be "strapped to the roof for the rest of the journey." We all smile politely as the driver issues the threat, but, to be honest, I don't think any of us has a clue what he's droning on about.

Instead, we sit there excitedly, and break open our packed lunches for the good stuff, but . . . nothing happens. We go nowhere. And out on the sidewalk there's a cluster of teachers scratching their chins and checking their watches. We know something is going on, and it can't be good because they're not saying a word to us. So when Miss D. gets on, looking unusually flustered, I ask if there's anything wrong.

"Well, we are running a little bit late, because one of the adults due to be coming to help has twisted her ankle, and without another responsible chaperone, I'm afraid we wouldn't be able to go."

There's an enormous groan of disappointment, but I'm not feeling it. No way. I'm not disappointed; I'm *freaking out*. What if we can't go? After all the hard work and bruises and near-death experiences? Are you kidding me?

It throws me so badly I think I'm going to be sick, and I wonder what the driver would do to me if I threw up in his pee-only bathroom. But just as I start searching for a paper bag to breathe into, Miss D. chirps up with the punch line.

"But it's all fine now. We've found, at the last minute, a replacement chaperone."

I punch the air, narrowly missing Giraffles.

"Now it's not another teacher, but I want all of you to act respectfully to our volunteer, just as you would anyone else."

There's an unusual force in her voice, and she seems to be looking at me a lot as she says it, with a strange expression on her face that seems to change from apologetic to forceful and back again, as if on rotation.

I don't get it. Why is she singling me out? I've never had detention in my life. If I wasn't so stoked at the fact that the trip's back on, I might even be a bit offended.

"Now some of you will know our knight in shining armor, so please can you give him a huge round of applause?"

Clapping fills the bus, and I join in—of course I do. But only momentarily, as our savior appears between the front seats.

And let me tell you, this is no knight.

It's a rat.

A lousy, stinking rat who's going to ruin my fun.

And his name . . . is Dylan.

12

Older brothers are put on this planet for one reason: to make life a pure torture.

All my life Dylan's been doing that. I swear, my earliest memory is of him leaning over my crib and rubbing his hands together before taking the pacifier from my mouth.

Since then, he's kicked me and punched me, drawn on me when I'm asleep, and told me I was the world's first living brain donor.

He's done everything in his power to make me his victim, and look at what he's done now: hijacked the one thing that I thought I might get some joy out of.

I'd write down a rude word for him right now, but he'd probably find a way of ruining that for me too. Make my pen squirt ink in my face or something.

Instead, I ignore him for the entire journey, despite the fact that I can feel him looking at me and hear him laughing.

Miss D. does come to talk to me, though, pulling me aside to tell me what happened.

"I can see that you're not very happy about this situation, Danny."

I shrug, which takes some restraint, since I actually want to scream **"THIS IS MY WORST NIGHTMARE BROUGHT TO LIFE!!!"**

"I know how much this trip means to you. More than anyone else in the whole class. And I know that your relationship with your brother isn't always the best . . ."

I raise my eyebrow so high it almost hits the roof of the bus.

". . . But believe me, Danny, I had no choice. It was Dylan or no trip. No one else could come on such short notice, and we needed a responsible adult to help out."

"Responsible? *Dyl?*" The words catch in my throat like I've tried to swallow a killer whale in one gulp. "He can't even spell the word, and he DEFINITELY doesn't know what it means. He puts pepper on my cornflakes and worms in my bed. He has the intellect of a mashed potato. I wouldn't put him in charge of a sunflower seed, never mind thirty of us!"

Miss D. does everything I expect of her. She smiles sadly and nods. It's like she can actually feel my pain. It's like she actually agrees with me. But then she also says this:

"He's eighteen years old, Danny. Which means he can help us. I promise I will not let him spoil your trip. You have my word."

I plaster a smile on my face and thank her. But she doesn't know Dyl like I do. He's slyer than a fox. I stare out the window, trying to preempt every bit of torture heading my way.

The next four hours drag by. Well, they do at first until we get out of the city, which is slow and painful work. I could walk faster on my hands than our bus moves for the first ninety minutes. In fact, it takes so long I expect it to get dark by the time we reach the great outdoors. But it doesn't. If anything, it gets lighter, and after staring confusedly for a while, I work out why: There are no apartment buildings blocking out the sun. No huge billboards or telephone poles either, just the occasional looming electrical tower.

It's weird, like I've just landed on the moon or something. It looks alien. And even though I'm safely tucked inside a comfy bus, with a "pee-only" toilet, I feel a bit weird too. Like I'm a long way from home. Like the rules outside are different from the ones I'm used to. The cars move quicker here. There are fewer traffic lights. And there's way fewer people, but more animals.

It seems like I'm not the only one feeling the change either. There's a kid in our class called Jonny Walker. He's all right, harmless enough, but for the last two years I don't think I've ever seen him with his head out of his phone. Until today, 'cause Miss D. has banned all screens until tonight, so poor Jonny is watching the world go by, his head twisting backward and forward so quickly it's like he's watching a game of tennis on double speed.

Anyway, about two hours in, Jonny spots a bunch of animals in the distance, grazing in a field, and I swear to you, no lie, he shouts:

"Look! Rhinos!"

And like a bunch of idiots we all spin around, to see . . . not rhinos, but cows.

It is, without a doubt, the stupidest thing I have ever heard in my life, but for a minute, a split second, we all think it's true.

Jonny blushes when he's called out on it. I'm pretty sure one of the cows even shakes her head as we sail past.

"*What?!*" says Jonny with a shrug. "Anyone could've made the same mistake. It's not like I've ever seen one before."

And that makes me think, 'cause you know what? It's the same for me—for most of us, probably. Foxes, yes; rats, occasionally. But cows? That aren't on a TV screen?

Nope.

So I do what I can to make him feel better. "Easy mistake to make," I say. "We've got a Giraffles *inside* the bus, so why not a rhino out there?"

And he laughs, and so does old Giraffles, and you know what? For a while I stop thinking about Dylan, who's still staring out the window, probably mistaking the cow for a stegosaurus.

Once we get there, I think to myself, it'll be fine.

And I think it so hard that it rolls around in my head on a loop, even when I manage to fall asleep against the window.

13

I wake with a start, Dyl screaming in my ear.

"FIRE!" he yells. **"SAVE YOURSELF! WOMEN, CHILDREN, AND IDIOT BROTHERS FIRST!"**

I know I shouldn't buy it. I've known him all my life, witnessed his practical jokes every day of my freaking existence, but I was dead asleep when he did it—drooling, and dreaming about climbing the world's biggest mountain. (Somehow I managed to do it without any kind of rope, like Bear Grylls crossed with Dumbledore.) So when Dyl sounds the foghorn in my ear, I jump instinctively out of my seat, cracking my head on the luggage rack above.

I crumple, half of my brain probably still clinging to the rack, and Dyl brays like a donkey, slapping Giraffles and MandM on the arms, reminding them of just how hilarious he is.

But because they've met him before, they actually know what a doofus he is, and turn instead to help me up.

"C'mon," says Marcus.

"We're here," says Maureen, which cheers me up to no end.

Even Miss D. isn't impressed with Dyl, giving him a look so sour it could turn milk to cheese in seconds.

I stumble from the bus, rubbing my head, taking in a couple of HUGE mountains in the distance, my ears hearing something that has to be a river. It gets my pulse racing, dreaming about the excitement that lies ahead.

But right outside the bus, there's not really a lot to see.

Perhaps I was expecting log cabins, or shacks at least, with little chimneys pumping smoke from them. Maybe I thought we'd be greeted by a team of buff-looking outdoorsy types too, but neither of these things are *anywhere* in sight.

All I *can* see is a pile of long canvas bags and a woman standing beside them, who at first sight appears to be around 132 years old. She's not stooped over or anything, far from it, she's standing bolt upright, almost as if she's on parade. But her face is crumpled like a ball of paper, her hair as thin as spiderwebs, and her arms . . . Well, they wouldn't look out of place on a snowman.

The second she opens her mouth, though, we know who's in charge.

"MY FRIENDS!" she booms, the force of her voice blowing us all back a pace or two. **"WELCOME TO WILD OUT!"** She has an accent that is impossible to place, though it is most definitely posh. Posh but properly friendly.

"My name is Geraldine Farquaharson-Smythe, though my friends and recruits"—and she points at us in turn—"call me Geri. I am the founder of this wonderful establishment." Again, she points a skeletal finger, this time at the field that surrounds us.

We turn as one, looking for what she's pointing at. Unless all the buildings are really well camouflaged, there is literally nothing to see.

"I wish I could explain to you fully about the

delights that are heading your way. I wish I could tell you fully about the perilous climbing, and mind-bending orienteering. I wish you could picture the river kayaking or zip-lining, but I don't have the words. All I can do is insist that you savor every moment that comes your way. It will test you physically and crazily, but you will NEVER forget it, you have my word! Now, you must be exhausted after such a long and arduous journey, but, worry not, I have a feast fit for the hungriest platoon waiting for you, just as soon as you build your accommodation. So, my new recruits, bend your backs, get to it, and soon you will be eating nothing but the freshest and finest cuisine we can offer."

Giraffles looks confused. "I didn't see a McDonald's on the way in, did you?" he whispers.

I shake my head. "There's probably a drive-through disguised as a tree or something," I say. Though, to be honest, I'm more confused about how the canvas sacks in front of us are possibly going to turn into a hotel.

Unlike the others, I have the sense to keep my mouth shut . . .

"Er . . . Miss D.?" asks Hannah Sycamore. "Are we sleeping on the bus or something?"

But before Miss D. can answer, Geri shakes her head and points a bony finger at the canvas sacks.

"What? The hotel's underground?" asks Rosie Sim, sparing Hannah's blushes but causing a rainbow of her own.

"No, *no*, my dear young thing," booms Geri. "Tents! In the bag there. Each tent sleeps three. So get to it. Last one to get theirs up is a rotten egg! And besides . . ." She stops, raises her head to the clouds, and sniffs, long and hard. ". . . There's a storm brewing."

Our eyes narrow in confusion, and I look up and sniff too, but only get a whiff of Dylan, who hasn't showered in the last six months.

"Best do as she says," I whisper to Giraffles, and we grab Lucky to share with us, because we know he's bound to have the best snacks in his bag, plus

100

there is NO WAY I am sharing with Dyl and his toxic feet.

We haul a bag from the pile, pull it to a flat piece of grass, and tip its contents at our feet, frowning at the endless poles, ropes, and canvas sheets that sit there.

"Where's the instructions?" I ask sensibly.

Giraffles searches, almost climbing inside the sack and wearing it as a ski mask before muffledly shouting, "There aren't any."

"Indeed there aren't," confirms Geri, appearing at our shoulders. "Missions don't come with a manual. So fire up your initiative and engage your instincts!"

She marches on, and we hear a whirring as she walks.

"Do you think that's her hearing aid making that noise?" I ask Lucky.

"Nah, more likely it's her electric hip."

Giraffles giggles. "It's not just her hip that's metallic. That Geri's not human. She can't be at her age. She's a cyborg, and that's her brain you can hear. Her brain and her titanium skeleton."

I weigh up Giraffles' theory as I watch her strut to the next group. Seems unlikely, I think, but I'm not going to rule anything out.

"We don't need instructions anyway," laughs Lucky, "'cause look who's got Google and unlimited data right here." He whips out a phone so swanky it looks like it belongs in a *Star Wars* movie.

His fingers flash across the screen, but the phone is not as speedy. In fact, nothing happens. The screen simply turns blank, apart from two words.

Two words that strike fear into city kids like us.

No signal.

Lucky turns pale and looks at us with dread in his eyes.

"I don't like this, you guys," he says with a shiver. "I think I want to go home."

14

The news spreads like wildfire.

There are wide eyes and slack jaws.

There are cries of dismay and a wave of phones being pulled from pockets because no one believes the rumors are true.

Jonny Walker actually falls to his knees and howls at the moon, which seems a bit over the top, to be honest, but I'm more concerned with working out what this mess of poles and canvas actually turns into. Plus the light is starting to fail, and old Geri doesn't look like the sort to bail you out just because it's getting dark and that's when the grizzly bears come out to play.

We make a start. Well, we do after we've looked at what everyone else is doing and we can copy them.

I even look to see how Dyl has tackled it, which makes me feel a bit sick inside. For some strange reason he has a three-person tent all to himself, but even without any help his tent is already upright and he's hammering in the pegs and ropes. He looks quite smug about it as well, standing at attention as Geri approaches and snapping out a salute. I decide to check with Mom when I get home to see if he was actually adopted.

"No need to salute, soldier," Geri barks. "You're not in the service yet."

"Won't be long, though, ma'am." Dyl doesn't let his salute drop, so Geri offers him a hand to shake instead.

"Well, let's see what you're made of these next few days, eh?" And she closes her grip around his.

The result is slow at first but builds quickly, like when you eat a red chili by mistake and your mouth gradually feels like it's been set on fire. I see it in Dyl's eyes. They narrow in confusion, then slowly, slowly widen as he realizes he's actually shaking hands with something resembling a boa constrictor.

I don't know if Geri's doing it because she's seen through our Dyl already, or just because she likes to test the strongest recruits, but she squeezes harder. And harder. And harder still, until it looks like Dyl is having trouble breathing. His fingertips have turned the purest white, but his face is kind of blue, and I'm imagining that his brain is racing, trying to work out how he's been taken down by a granny from the Iron Age.

"Can you hear that?" whispers Giraffles. "Her hand, it's whirring again . . . I swear that Geri is pure robot."

"Then let's get this flippin' tent up before she tries to shake anything that's attached to our bodies."

So we try. Really we do, for what seems like hours. And we do manage to make some things, but *none* of them are tents.

We create a canoe (kind of), a 1975 Volkswagen Beetle (if you use your imagination), and if you squint your eyes up really tight we seem to create a life-sized version of the Statue of Liberty.

But seeing as none of them are a tent, and none of them use every single piece of the kit in the bag, we realize we've not quite got it right and have to start over again.

Finally, after much wailing, arguing, and innocent cheating by inspecting everyone else's efforts, we have something that resembles a tent. There's still one spare pole left (annoyingly), but we pretend it never existed and ram it back inside the bag.

"I'm going in," says Giraffles excitedly, and he folds his long limbs inside, only to start banging the sides of the tent repeatedly, like he's trying to swat a particularly annoying fly.

"What are you doing?" I yell.

"I'm looking for the light switch," he replies. "It's dark in here!"

I laugh. I laugh like I've never laughed before, not even that time when Dyl tried to wash his legs in the toilet and then got stuck when he accidentally flushed it. And what makes it even better is that Lucky is as confused as Giraffles.

"You're kidding me?" he yells. "It must be in there." And he dives in too, with much thrashing and confusion.

"Never mind the light switch," Lucky shouts. "I can't find the power outlet either, or the Wi-Fi box."

"And where are the beds?" adds Giraffles, just as Geri approaches. She smiles, but shakes her head.

"I think they might be in for a shock," she says to me.

"Don't think they've ever slept in a tent," I reply.

"And what about you, Danny?"

"Oh yeah," I lie. "All the time."

She stares at me, hard. And I swear I hear a whirring as her eyeballs narrow, like they're drilling into my brain, searching for the truth.

"I'd, er . . . I'd better explain to them what a sleeping bag is," I stammer. Though to be honest, I'm not exactly sure either.

I'm not sure about much anymore. But I'm sure it'll all seem better in the morning . . .

I woke up super early.

So early I never actually went to sleep—how could I when the outdoors is so flipping noisy?

All night there were grunts and groans and snuffles and wails, but only 37 percent of those came from inside the tent (though some of those noises smelled rank).

I have no idea what was prowling around outside, but I'm glad Jonny Walker wasn't in our tent, 'cause in his head it was probably a T-rex and a raptor having a party.

Got to admit, though, that by three a.m. my sleep-deprived imagination was going a bit crazy too. I'm sure at some point I heard Dylan out there, wrestling with whatever was on the prowl, and I felt relief in the fact that the stegosaurus was probably going to rip him limb from limb.

"Euuuurghhhhhh," comes a noise from Lucky's sleeping bag, and for once it doesn't seem to be coming from his backside. "I have not slept a wink all night."

"Your butt's been wide awake, believe me," I reply.

"It's this mattress, Dan, it's like sleeping on a stale cookie."

My tummy rumbles at the mention of food. We'd all been too tired to do anything but crawl inside our tents when we'd finished setting them up and although Lucky had tons of candy in his bag, there wasn't enough to stop me from being as hungry as I was tired.

So after wrestling with the zipper for what feels like an eternity, I fall out of the tent to be confronted with a horde of the roughest-looking zombies imaginable, who are, in fact, just my classmates who have had as little sleep as me.

Many of them don't have bags under their eyes as much as suitcases, while poor Jonny Walker is on his knees, weeping onto his mobile phone.

"I just don't understand," he wails. "How can there be no signal?"

It's not a conversation I want to get involved with, so I give him a wide berth, and instead accidentally fall into the clutches of Dyl, who is doing chin-ups from a tree so old that it looks like it was planted when a caveman spat out an acorn because of a nut allergy.

Dylan greets me in a typical way.

"Sleep well, loser?"

"Thought you were exercising your body, not your tiny mind," I reply, used to our morning routine.

"This beautiful body has already run six miles this morning. What exercise have you done?"

I think about telling him I had survived a deadly

111

gas attack, thanks to Lucky's rotten guts, but I'm so hungry I stop myself and head instead to the others, who are grouped around a long, narrow table, with tree trunks for chairs.

"What's for breakfast?" I ask, as there's no sign of any Cocoa Puffs. Or Lucky Charms. Not even a Frosted Flake. Just a pile of spoons, bowls, and a load of old tin buckets.

We don't have long to wait though, as Geri shouts from behind us.

"My lovely recruits . . . breakfast is served!"

We spin around, hopeful for cereal, toast, or even some fruit if we have to, but—no, oh no— Geri is walking toward us flanked by a couple of the BIGGEST beasts I have ever seen.

"COWS?" I yell, before Jonny can shout "rhino" or "tiger" or something equally stupid.

They're scary somehow. How did they get so wide? And one of them is pure white (apart from random dark splotches that I can only guess are poop), while the other is dark, dark brown.

"We're having burgers?" says Giraffles. "For breakfast?"

"Don't be ridiculous," replies Marcus, before Maureen adds, "Burgers aren't made of cows. They're made of meat."

"Yeah, but the meat has got to come from somewhere, so where does it come from, eh?"

Neither M nor M has an answer to that, though Jonny tries to find out the answer on his phone before he gets yet another painful reminder of the signal problem.

Thankfully, old Geri comes to the rescue. "You all make an excellent point: Too often we eat and drink things without a clue about where the food comes from. Well, not today! In fact, not while you are here at all. Burgers DO often come from cows"— at this, MandM look on the verge of passing out in shock—"but we will not be eating Flossy and Rossy here, we will simply be milking them. Or at least, you will."

"For what?" asks Jonny, with a completely straight face, which even shocks Geri.

"Well, for the milk."

"Oh." Jonny grins like a light bulb went off in his head. He pauses, nods, then adds:

"So where's the pink one, then?"

"The pink what?"

"The pink cow."

Geri looks, well, confused, and, for the first time, a bit irritated. "Why would we have a pink cow?"

Now it's Jonny's turn to look at her like she's nuts. "Well, it's obvious, isn't it? The white cow is vanilla, the brown one gives chocolate. So where's the pink cow, 'cause I'd like a strawberry milkshake?"

Jonny stops talking and there's silence. Deafening, tumbleweed silence.

And then laughter.

Loads of it.

So much laughter that poor old Jonny turns redder than a scarlet cow. So red that I almost wish he was a cow, so we could have the finest raspberry milkshake the world has ever tasted.

16

Never in my life will I ever again walk past a supermarket without running up to it and hugging it like it was my mom.

For the past two hours I would have given anything for a corner shop, never mind a full-sized one. I can see their fridges now, with more milk than you can imagine: two percent, skim, whole. Heck, right now I am SO HUNGRY I would even drink almond milk (whatever that is).

It's been ridiculous, emotional, tiring. I don't know how I thought farmers got milk out of cows—I'm sure they've got machines that help, but Geri wasn't having any of that.

"The only machines you need are these things," she says, as she wiggles her arthritic fingers before showing us how to use them as pumps on the cows' udders. Cue much yelling of:

"EUGH!"
"GROSS!"
"I AM NOT TOUCHING THAT!"

But
I don't
mind, and
anyway
the milk
pours out
at such a
rate when
she touches
them that
I'm convinced
there's actually a

hidden tap she's turned to get it flowing.

"I'll have a go," I say, when she asks for volunteers, and I sit on the wobbly, wooden stool that she places next to Flossy (or is it Rossy? It doesn't really matter either way).

"Now don't be shy," she says. "Their udders aren't as sensitive as they look, so you can afford to grip tightly."

I do as she says, flinching as my hands wrap around what looks like an overinflated rubber glove. With every muscle in my body tense, and my eyes welded shut in a grimace, I pull, and . . .

Nothing.

I pull again. Harder.

Still nothing.

So I try once more, though I presume I may have been a little too rough, because the cow bucks like a rodeo horse, kicking the steel bucket with more force than a Ronaldo free kick so it narrowly misses the right of Dyl's head.

"Do that again and you're dead!" he hisses, and

I make a note to pull slightly to the left next time. Well, I would if I wasn't traumatized by what just happened.

"Let's give someone else a chance, shall we?" Geri smiles through gritted teeth. But everyone else is just as bad as me.

Giraffles can't tease out a drop, and neither can MandM, despite milking Flossy and Rossy at the same flipping time. Jonny is terrible at it, probably because he's holding his phone at the same time, and even Lucky comes up short. In fact, his efforts make Rossy empty her guts.

"Good luck putting that on your cereal," sneers Dyl, before pushing Lucky aside and sitting on the stool. "Time to watch a master at work . . ." He cracks his knuckles, blows on them, and wraps his fingers around the udder, moving with the speed and precision of a concert pianist.

Instantly, we hear a noise. A faint tinkling, which reminds us with a thump to the head just how beyond hungry we are. We bend down to see a thin jet of liquid hitting the inside of the bucket.

"What is that?!" yells Jonny, like it's the most disgusting thing he has ever seen in his life.

"It's milk, you idiot!" we yell as one, before we break into a weird kind of rain dance. Except it's not a rain dance, it's a milk dance. And I know I shouldn't be celebrating, 'cause it's Dyl who's made it rain after all, but right now I want breakfast more than I've ever wanted anything in my life. So as long as he doesn't gloat or milk his success (sorry) too badly, I'm prepared to overlook it.

In fact, his success makes me even more determined to make it work myself, so I grab a stool, park myself beside Rossy, and pull and pump until finally, FINALLY, I get some milk out of her swollen udder.

It's not a torrent. It's barely even a trickle, to be honest, but it's my trickle, and I did it without the use of Google. And when I taste the cereal that I've made with way too little (but incredibly fresh) milk? I'm telling you, it's the BEST thing I have eaten in my entire life. Even when Dyl sneezes in it on purpose, he doesn't spoil it.

I eat it all. You bet I do. Because if this morning is anything to go by, I'm going to need every bit of energy I can get.

17

So I've eaten, kind of. And even though it was hardly a feast, I'm ready. You know, to climb stuff, and jump off stuff, or even fall off stuff (which is way more likely, given my career as a free runner so far).

But two minutes into stuffing my backpack for the day I feel a rumble in my stomach that isn't hunger. I need to . . . go.

No, not home—no way.

You know . . . go.

And I realize I have no idea where the bathroom even is, but I'd better find out STAT.

I duck out of the tent, failing to stay on my feet yet again, which doesn't help the fact that I now really need to go.

I see MandM walking toward me, and for some reason it pops into my head to ask them what they do when one of them needs to use the bathroom. Surely they separate long enough for that to happen, but does one of them wait outside the bathroom door? Fortunately, another twinge in my belly forces the thought from my head.

"Where's the bathroom?" I ask, doing the "I need the toilet" run, which involves clamping your butt cheeks so firmly closed that you only move from the knees down.

They both point toward it with such certainty that it makes me think maybe they DO go to the bathroom at the same time, but I shake off that thought and waddle urgently to a small but tall tent at the far end of the field.

It's nothing like any kind of public toilet I've ever seen before, but I'm that desperate that I push the canvas aside and step straight in, only for my nostrils to be attacked by the most putrid, nose-melting whiff I have ever smelled in my life—and I know what evil smells like: It smells like Dylan.

The tent is tiny, so it only takes me three-tenths of a second to work out what smells, and it's the toilet itself. Well, I say the toilet. It isn't a toilet. It's a bucket. With a trash bag inside and a toilet seat balanced precariously on top.

As if that isn't bad enough, there's no flush! Now I'm no snob, I live in a building with, like, a million other people, and some of those people have questionable hygiene, but I bet you that every single one of those people has a flushable toilet, and that they wouldn't share that toilet with the rest of their class—and their caveman of a brother—if it didn't flippin' flush.

I tell myself not to look in the bucket.

Don't look don't look don't look don't look . . .

But then I look, of course I do, and my stomach flips and lurches and my breakfast does the same, and I have no option but to turn around and sit down—all without falling off the bucket.

But don't worry, that's where the detail stops, because I do what I need to do, and feel such a surge of relief when I've finished, and no one—in particular, me—died.

So I look for the toilet paper, 'cause the sooner that's done the sooner I can breathe fresh air and delete the memory that this ever even happened.

But the thing is, there is no paper.

Not a piece, a shred, a particle. In fact, in horror

I realize that there probably wasn't any to start with, 'cause there are no empty cardboard rolls there either, not even on the floor.

And I start to panic. Wouldn't you? All I want to do is get out of here and climb a freaking mountain but I can't, because of the obvious.

So I do what any self-respecting, but slightly panicking eleven-year-old would do:

I shout for my best friend.

"GIRAAAAAAAFLLLEEEEEEEES!!!" I yell, so loudly that I'm sure a pack of actual giraffes in Africa hears me as well as the human one I'm calling.

There's no reply. So I call again. And again. And again. In fact, I call so many times that I'm in danger of losing my voice, and I start to fear that I might die of suffocation or toxic shock or something.

I feel like one of those people clinging to an iceberg after the *Titanic* had gone down, except it's boiling hot in here now and the only way I'm going to drown is in my own sweat.

And then, just when I think all hope is lost, I hear him, like a heavenly angel with a super-long neck.

"Danny? That you in there? You OK?"

"Don't come in!" I gasp, then realize that no one with half a brain cell would even consider it.

"Giraffles, bro. Disaster. There's no toilet paper in here."

There's a pause, then, "So what do you wipe your butt on?"

"That's why I'm calling you. What do I do?"

"Well, I don't know, do I?"

"Have you got any?"

"Any what?"

"Toilet paper, you idiot!"

There's an agonizing pause.

"No . . . but I have got this," and his hand appears through the canvas slit, holding the grossest piece of tissue you have ever seen in your life. It looks like he's been blowing his nose in it, and everyone else has for that matter, for the last nine and a half years.

"I can't use that!" I squeal.

"Well, that's all I've got."

"Then go and ask Geri for some, will you? Quick! It stinks in here."

I hear him amble away, muttering, "Too much information," as he goes.

And he's gone for hours. Or it could actually only be a minute, but it feels like hours and when he comes back, the news is not good.

"She says she doesn't have any. Says we have to use a dock leaf, whatever that is. Oh, and she also says, whatever you do, don't use a nettle, 'cause apparently nature often makes them grow next to each other. Fascinating, that, eh? I had no idea, did y—"

"PLEASE," I squeal, **"PLEASE, FOR THE SAKE OF MY NOSE, GET ME A DOCK LEAF, QUICK! IN FACT, GET ME THREE!"**

I wait again. Eyes stinging, hope fading, mood falling, until finally, FINALLY, a hairy hand appears through the slit, clutching a tote bag loaded with leaves.

I look inside, frowning. I've never seen a dock leaf in my life, but these look a bit, I don't know, spiky . . .

"Bro, are you sure these are the right ones?" I ask.

The hand gives me a thumbs-up.

"Did you check with Geri?"

Two hands appear, both of them giving me a thumb.

I wonder why he's not talking anymore, then a wave of embarrassment hits me: It must be the smell. It's obviously killing him, and I feel so ashamed but also grateful that he would do this for me that I shove my hand into the bag, grab a few of the leaves, and use them.

What a relief. I'll be out in seconds . . . Nearly . . .

"AAAAAARGHHHHHHHH!"

I don't know what starts to sting first, my hand or my butt; in fact, it doesn't even matter. All that matters is that I'm in pain. Red-hot agony. Agony that cannot be ignored. In a second I'm on my feet with the bucket lying on its side, and it's all my fault. Not that I care—all I care about is the fact that my butt (and my hand) is on fire, and unless I find water, quickly, someone is going to have to call the fire department.

Without thinking, I dash from the tent, not knowing, never mind caring, that my pants are still around my ankles.

I waddle in circles, falling occasionally, squealing repeatedly for WATER!

There are gasps, cries, and laughter. And of course, who is laughing loudest?

Not Giraffles, 'cause he's just appeared out of the trees, looking shocked, clutching a load of leaves so soft they sort of look like they're made of kitten fur.

It's Dylan. Laughing so loud he's bent over sideways, wheezing.

And where is he standing? Right by the toilet tent, him and the hairy hands that passed me the bag in the first place.

I want to hurt him. I want to humiliate him. I want to . . .

STOP MY BUTT FROM BURNING!

So, as much as it pains me, I ignore my idiot of a brother, and go running in the direction of Miss D., who by now seems to be trembling. And covering her eyes.

18

By late afternoon, day one of the single greatest trip of my life, the only thing that is going wild is my bottom.

Actually, that's not true. Every other kid in my class, plus my demonic cretin of a brother, is going wild right this second, climbing a rock face. The torture starts as I lie in the tent, ice pack on butt, forced to listen as Geri talks about the day ahead.

"Recruits. It may be day one, but on my word this is no easy introduction. Rock climbing demands so much. Strength, stamina, and a sharp, analytical mind. And believe me, you will need all of this if you are to conquer the rock I'm going to put in front of you. It will be tough. Your body and your brain will ache by the end, but the views from the top will make it all worthwhile, believe me."

These are hardly words to cheer me up, and it's made worse when I hear them excitedly gathering their stuff. Giraffles and Lucky look sheepish when they pop back into the tent for their backpacks.

Strangely enough, neither of them volunteers to stay behind with me. Not that I blame them.

But this is nothing compared to the torture that follows. Hours and hours of hearing them whoop and yell and laugh.

I can hear it despite burying my head below every sleeping bag, roll mat, and pillow that I can find in our tent.

"Stupid tent . . ." I groan. "Stupid tent with its stupid flimsy walls that aren't even walls 'cause they're not even made out of bricks . . ."

It's fair to say that I might be feeling a teensy bit sorry for myself, but you would too if you were me. I mean, when was the last time you had to tell your favorite teacher and a retired drill sergeant that you're in agony 'cause you just wiped your butt with a load of nettles?

When was the last time you were in so much agony and in fear of having your butt amputated, yet wouldn't dare let any of the staff inspect the damage 'cause you'd die of embarrassment if they did?

And when was the last time your older brother told all your classmates that you'd done it on purpose, not just to get sympathy but also because you've got a rare brain disease that makes you addicted to butt pain?

Not lately, I'd imagine, so forgive me if I'm a teeny-tiny bit upset.

All I can do is lie here, without moving a muscle—especially a butt muscle—'cause if I do, the ice pack balanced on my injuries falls off and I have to shout for help to get it placed securely on the cheeks again. Oh yeah, this really is the gift that keeps on giving . . .

So I lie here, thinking of ways of getting my revenge that don't involve:

A. Killing Dyl stone dead

B. Going to prison, and/or

C. Upsetting Mom.

While at the same time causing Dyl the maximum amounts of both physical and mental pain. But as it turns out, I'm not that good at revenge—certainly nowhere near as good as him anyway. As soon as I let my imagination go, it gets grisly and he ends up being ripped to shreds by a rhino that I hire from a local zoo, which leads straight to point A coming true, followed by B and C toppling like dominoes.

So after hours dedicated to trying, I give up and try to concentrate my mind on both healing and making the most of the two days that I have left. As soon as my butt heals anyway.

Who knows, maybe my bruised backside will

become an asset. Aren't there monkeys in Africa that use theirs as a warning beacon to ward off predators?

Maybe I made that up. I don't know. I don't know much about anything anymore. Maybe I'm just going out of my mind with boredom.

But what I do know is that I'll fight back from this. And if I can clobber Dyl along the way?

Then.

Bring.

It.

On.

There were two full moons last night. One shining down outside the tent, and a swollen one inside, keeping me awake, along with the hyenas and bears snuffling around outside.

But as the sun subs in for the moon, I make up my mind to be positive.

We've got two days left, and I'm not going to let damaged cheeks or a prankster brother spoil either of them.

So I'm up first, exiting the tent without tripping, and getting to the toilet tent before anyone else can do something unthinkable in it.

On the way, I bump into Miss D.

"You all right, Danny?" She smiles, but not in an "I'm laughing at you" way. It's clearly more of a "you poor thing, having a blistered backside and a psycho for a brother" kind of way. Which I appreciate. And agree with.

I only nod though. I'm happy to rant about Dyl, but don't really want to get into a conversation about the other bit. I'd rather pretend that it never happened, and I imagine Miss D. feels the same.

Anyway, I'm about to push on to find a real bona fide dock leaf, when she does the kindest thing imaginable, the kind of thing that sums up why she completely and utterly rocks. She hands me a packet of tissues.

"I thought you might not be in the mood for foraging this morning." She winks, and moves on, leaving me to murmur, "Thank you," while trying not to cry like a fool.

And, you know what? That spurs me on even

further. I practically skip into the bathroom tent (being careful not to face-plant into the bucket) and emerge feeling like I could climb anything put in front of me.

Breakfast is next and I manage to pull enough milk from Flossy without giving myself blisters, and we even have time for a Jonny classic, when Geri reveals a load of hens living in the next field, ready to gift us eggs to cook.

But Jonny looks terrified and blurts, without thinking, "But how on earth do you milk a chicken?"

Now I don't want to sound harsh, but it's the funniest and dumbest thing I've ever heard in my life, and it gives me confidence, 'cause I know that for the rest of the day people won't be just giggling about my idiocy.

So when Geri tells us about what the day holds, I am properly excited for it.

"MORNING, TROOPS," she barks, with an impressive enthusiasm for someone who fought in the Civil War. "I hope you slept well, because today is going to be a challenge. Tomorrow, we will embark on our final expedition, so to harden your resolve and put muscle on every bone in your body, I am going to test you. First of all, armed only with a compass and map, you will be orienteering—"

"What's paper folding got to do with anything?" Giraffles whispers, deadly serious.

"That's origami, you nugget."

"Oh right," he says, though I know he's still none the wiser.

"Trekking from this point, and avoiding any obstacles in front of you, you will proceed to the river, where we will pick up kayaks and paddle to the final checkpoint. There, you will find a feast awaiting you. There will be challenges, there will be tears, but by the end of it, every single one of you will feel like a champion. So good luck . . . and steel yourselves."

We turn to a pile of alien-looking equipment to our left, confused looks on our faces. First, there are a series of square metallic boxes with glass screens and maps inside. At least I think they're maps. They just look like a load of random squiggles and shapes to me.

Lucky picks one up and stares at it, flipping it around and frowning.

"What are you looking for?" I ask.

"The serial number," he says. "It looks ancient. And this is either a very old model or it's just not working."

"It's not an iPad, you fool. It's a map that's been laminated," I tell him.

"Yeah, I knew that." He blushes, though he's not the only one to make the same mistake. I swear I see Jonny pinching at his screen with his thumb and index finger, trying to make the map bigger.

I choose not to tell him though. I don't want to draw attention to him when he's still blushing about milking a flipping chicken.

Next to the maps are a load of clear plastic blocks, smaller this time so they fit snugly in your hand, with lines coming off them and the letters *N*, *E*, *S*, and *W*.

"These look like those things from *Star Trek*," blurts Marcus.

"Yeah," adds Maureen, "Kirk speaks to that Scottish dude on them, the one who's always blowing up the engine on the ship."

"BEAM ME UP, SCOTTY!" they both shout into the plastic.

"Hhhhhhm, unlikely," says Giraffles, though he clearly has no idea what they do either, and I only know 'cause I've seen Dyl messing with one after coming home from a Scouts trip.

"It's a compass," I say. "It tells you which way

to go: north, south, east, west . . . you know . . ."

They shrug, bemused.

"Explorers use 'em."

They shrug again.

"It's like GPS . . ." I add.

"Ahhhhh." They nod, all three idiots together. "I seeeeee . . . So where's the power button?"

I could, at this point, shake my head and walk away in disgust, but I remember how supportive they were over Wipegate. If they laughed, they at least didn't do it to my face. So I grin through clenched teeth and explain how it all works, in brilliant, clear detail.

I tell them about how the earth is a huge magnet and how the north end of the compass is drawn to align with its magnetic field. I do it brilliantly, in fact I feel like a teacher, like how Miss D. must feel, all smart and proud.

And do you know what they do?

They laugh at me, and tell me the nettles must've rotted my brain.

So I do the decent thing, and tell them something they will believe.

"No, you're right. Harry Potter invented them. Or Dumbledore did at least. It's all magic."

"Sounds more likely," Giraffles adds, and the others nod.

Maybe it's going to be harder to stay positive than I thought . . .

And so we're off, though where we are actually off to isn't quite so clear.

I can see the river on the map, but between us and that point, there are a LOT of squiggly lines that look like they've been drawn excitedly by a toddler who's just eaten the BIGGEST bag of candy.

Bemused by where to even start, we do what any novice explorers would—we watch what direction Dylan heads off in, and follow him.

He's chosen to work on his own (no surprise

given the fact that he's a power-crazed meathead with only one friend, who happens to live in a mirror), and despite the fact that he's only on this freaking trip to supposedly look after us, he clearly wants to get there first and win the race. Which he will of course, because he's the only one who knows that the compass wasn't actually invented at Hogwarts.

Within two minutes, he's out of sight, and we're left to flip between staring blindly at the compass, and then the map.

Our group is bigger than what is probably sensible. There's me, Giraffles, MandM, Lucky, plus Jonny, who I took pity on when no one wanted him in their group. After two minutes, I can kind of understand why.

"OOH. OOH. OOH." he shouts suddenly, after almost sticking his nose into the map. "Here," he points. **"HERE HERE HERE! WE HAVE TO GO HERE."**

Giraffles is irritated already. "I think Jonny might have spotted something he likes."

I give him a gentle dig and ask Jonny what he's seen.

"It's the answer to everything," he beams. "Look, the map says 'FB.' Right there. And you know what that means, don't you?"

"No," we all reply, as one.

"Well, 'FB' stands for Facebook, doesn't it? So there must be a phone tower there, where we can pick up a signal. We could call an Uber to give us a lift to the river. We might even get there before Dylan."

Now I'm no expert, but somehow I don't think Jonny's got that quite right, so I open the map and look for a list of what the symbols mean.

"Yeah . . . well, it's a nice thought, bro, but 'FB' means 'footbridge' . . ."

Cue multiple cries of, **"YOU DUMMY!"** from the others. At Jonny, not me.

"And before you ask," I add, "that 'i' isn't an iPhone-charging point either. It means 'information.'"

But Jonny isn't disheartened by this. If anything

he looks pleased with himself. "Maybe the people there can order us a car, then. They might even have Wi-Fi, you never know."

I walk on, before the temptation to bury his head in a pile of leaves gets too great.

We wander on for ages, and it doesn't take long until people start bickering about which is the right way. Even MandM disagree on whether left is best or not, which makes me realize just how lost we are.

But then, just when all hope is lost and I consider sending up an SOS flare (well, I do until I realize we clearly don't own one), we see hope up ahead.

It's Dyl, about fifty yards to our right.

"What's he doing there?" I ask.

"Maybe he's lost too?" says Giraffles.

"Impossible," I say. "He's way too annoying to ever let that happen."

"I don't even care," say MandM together. "I'm following him."

150

So we all do, except I do it way more cautiously than the others, because the difference is, I know him. I've had eleven years as his brother, so I know full well that he would NEVER let us follow him . . . unless he was up to something.

"Nettles were just a starter," I say out loud without even realizing. "And whatever main course Dyl's cooking up, I ain't eating it."

The others look at me like I'm a crazy person who won't shut up, no matter how loudly I warn them, so I stay a step behind. If they want to walk into his trap, then they can do it first, not me.

It doesn't take long to be proven right either. We push on through a particularly thick piece of forest: It's dark, with endless branches blocking out the light.

"It's OK," says Giraffles, hacking at the last bits of undergrowth with a stray dead twig. "We're nearly through the worst of it."

These turn out to be famous last words, because, as he swishes at the last branch, he triggers a booby

trap and up from nowhere springs the most evil-looking scarecrow you have ever seen in your whole life. It's naked, for starters, which doesn't help, but somehow, in practically no time at all, Dyl has built a figure entirely out of branches and twigs, all tied together with ivy. It stands over six feet high and, despite having no face, it is the scariest thing I have ever seen: Its long arms loom over us like a zombie.

"ARGGGGHHHHHH!" cries Giraffles.

"NOOOOOOOOOOOOO!" yell MandM, while Jonny breaks wind with such a savage blast that I know it's the worst kind of fart: the messy kind.

But I don't flinch, or even blink. I'm prepared. I have seen evil every day of my life, so when it appears, I'm ready for it.

"You'll have to do better than THAT, Dylan!" I yell into the trees.

And for the next twenty minutes, he tries his utmost: Things tap us on the shoulders, but when we turn around there's no one there; we're pelted with acorns from all angles, but when we try to throw some back there is no one to aim at; our ears are peppered with calls and wails that could either come from the most ferocious, dangerous animals on the planet, or from the lips of the biggest irritant that ever slimed his way across the earth.

By the end of it, even I'm starting to feel edgy, until I see, like a mirage in front of me, a break in the tree line, and beyond it a pile of kayaks; and, even better than that, I can hear the faint gurgling of a river (which makes me instantly need to pee, but it's OK, I can live with that).

I break into a dance of joy, somewhere between the floss and the sort of dancing your mom does at a wedding after too many glasses of wine, and I skip toward the clearing. I don't care if I'm first or not. I don't care if I get a kayak with more holes in it than a cheese grater. All I care about is not falling foul of Dylan . . . again.

And it's actually that last thought that stops my dancing. It's that thought that makes the others stop dancing too. Instead I hold my arms out wide to stop them from getting past me.

"Wait!" I whisper.

"What?" they reply.

"It's too easy. There's no way Dyl would let us get to the end without nailing us. He's too evil for that . . ." And that's when I see it. The most pathetic excuse for a disguised trap ever.

There, on the ground, right on the edge of the woods, is a huge rug of twigs, dead branches, and leaves. And the second I see it, I know that lurking below is a Danny-shaped hole, dug by my own brother's hands.

It's so obvious and so pathetic that I laugh out loud; in fact I howl, doubling over with my hands on my knees.

"I've seen through you—you and your terrible pathetic trap!" I shout.

And with the greatest of care, I lead my friends around the side of the "pit" to safety, and toward the majesty of the river.

But, in that one simple side step, I realize my fatal error: The blanket of twigs left for me is simply that. A blanket. There is no pit beneath.

I realize this when my feet are suddenly whipped out from beneath me, and I'm launched skyward and upside down, attached to a bungee rope that Dyl has hidden beneath a dense coil of ivy.

The blood races to my head, and it's a rush; of course it is. How could being thrown thirty feet in the air not be? But it's not the rush I wanted. And although the view from the top of the tallest tree should be epic, it is most definitely not. Because all I can see as I look down is my big brother, laughing his head off. And others in my class joining in too.

21

Nothing stops your butt from stinging like being unexpectedly thrown thirty feet into the air. Honestly, it's true. It makes your pride throb a bit, though.

Everyone had a good laugh, until they realized it wasn't going to be so easy to get me down, and Geri had to climb up to make sure I didn't fall on my head.

Can't say it did a lot for my confidence, listening to her motorized skeleton whirring its way toward me. No one really wants to be rescued by a person fifteen times their age, do they?

Still, better her than Dylan, and, believe me, he volunteered, only to be shot down by an icy glare from Miss D.

They couldn't pin it on him, of course. There were no security cameras out in the middle of nowhere, and Dyl is as good at lying as he is at being a scumbucket.

Put it this way, if it were his job, he'd be a billionaire by now.

Anyway, to cut a long and devastatingly embarrassing story short, I ended up getting a piggyback ride down from Geri, before she took Miss D. aside for a chat.

This just makes me feel even worse. I mean, it's not my

fault my brother is a psycho. Why can't he single someone else out instead of me?

This, and the nettles fiasco, only happened to me—and who knew how long it would take before I was singled out again?

I tried not to think about it as I munched on a soggy egg sandwich, but wasn't helped by Miss D., who called me aside.

"Danny, I'm worried."

"Me too," I said.

"I need you to stay away from Dylan."

"Believe me, I'm trying!"

"I appreciate that, but I need you to try harder. Now, I really don't know what's going on between you, but I've just had Geri in my ear, and she is more than a little concerned."

"Then tell Dyl, not me!" I pleaded. "He's tricking me, again and again."

"I'm telling you the same thing I've already told your brother. The reputation of the school is on the line. But, more important than that, I have to keep

161

you all safe. And I can't do that if you and Dylan are engaged in some kind of deathmatch."

"But, Miss—"

"But nothing. Give him a wide berth, Danny, that's all I'm asking."

There's nothing I could say to that, but it was still on my mind as Giraffles and I clambered into our kayak, ready for phase two of the day. The only positive was that I stopped thinking about it as soon as I sat down in the cold, wet boat. My butt cheeks hurt too much for me to worry about anything else.

Turns out Giraffles had things on his mind though.

"Er, Geri," he says apologetically. "Shouldn't we be wearing life vests or something?"

Seems sensible to me.

Geri, however, thinks otherwise.

"My dear boy, I've been bringing recruits down this river for decades now, and I've never lost a soldier yet. Should you fall out, just swim to the

162

surface. You can swim, can't you?"

Giraffles nods, and that's all Geri needs to move swiftly on.

"The mission is a simple one. Navigate your way downriver as quickly BUT AS SAFELY as possible"—and I know this is aimed at me—"and there are two things that you need to avoid at all costs. Firstly, this river is a nesting ground for the lesser spotted orange-crested warbler, a bird whose numbers have been falling in recent years. It is critical, CRITICAL, that you—like any good intrepid explorer—respect their habitat and do not disturb their nests! This is an important time for their young, and without them, the orange-crested warbler has no future."

There's a concerned murmur among the ranks, until Jonny pipes up with "What color are they? So we know what to look out for?"

Honestly, if he keeps going on like this we'll have enough material for a book before we get home. Geri very sensibly pretends he doesn't exist and carries on to point two, which is . . .

"Rapids! They're called that for a reason"—Jonny goes to open his mouth, but isn't quick enough—"and that's because they are quicker and more deadly than any roller coaster you've ever ridden. These rapids here would test even the most accomplished of adrenaline junkies, so I'm telling you now: Stay clear of them. They are well marked, so if you like your limbs attached to your bodies, then keep your senses about you and do what the signs tell you. Now, go and look after your partner, and we'll see you at the final checkpoint."

As warnings go, it's pretty clear, and as Giraffles and I push out from the bank I have no doubt about the fact that I'll be doing two things:

1. Exactly what Geri and Miss D. told us.

2. Not letting our Dylan anywhere near me.

As long as I do that, there's no way he can set me up.

And at first, this goes according to plan. In fact, it goes better than that, because guess what. Giraffles and I turn out to be kayaking heroes. This could, of course, come down to my long-limbed friend and his epically telescopic arms that propel us downriver at a wild pace; but I'd like to think I'm doing my part too, keeping us in rhythm and far away from the riverbank.

It's going so well that, actually, for a while we're at the front of the pack, waving to the imaginary crowds that line the bank. But after ten minutes or so, we feel two other kayaks drawing alongside us, and I know full well who one of them will belong to. It's Dyl, of course, which sets my heart racing and my bruised cheeks twitching. But then I see who's in the second boat, and it's Geri, powering her twig arms along at a furious rate (seriously, her paddles are more muscular). And that makes me feel way better, and safer too.

So we glide on, cutting the water in two, giving even the quickest of fish below us a serious, serious race.

Until . . .

"Hey, Danny. Look up there—is that Dylan waiting for us?"

I knew it. What he's done to Geri I've no idea. Drowned her probably, or thrown her off the nearest waterfall, before he does the same to me; but as we draw closer, I see his plan up close and personal, and it's obvious—almost pitiful—what he's trying to do.

"Look, Giraffles," I say, "look where he's stopped. Right by the sign to the rapids."

He looks and nods, 'cause it's true. Dyl has parked himself up at a small island in the middle of the river, where the water forks off in two different directions. And dug into the island is a wooden sign showing which way people go for the rapids.

Instantly, INSTANTLY, I am wise to his plan.

"I AM NOT FALLING FOR THIS!" I yell, full of anger.

"Falling for what?"

"Isn't it obvious? He's changed the direction of the sign, hasn't he? He's pointed it in the wrong way, so we maim ourselves on the rapids. As soon as we go past, he'll change it back again so everyone else is safe."

"You sure?"

I look to my brother: my nemesis, my über-archest enemy, put on this planet to make my life miserable hell. His face is stony, giving nothing away. But at that moment I can see into his brain, can visualize the evil pumping around his bloodstream.

"I am positive. Certain. Sure."

"And he's definitely not trying to double-bluff us?"

"That would involve his current brain cell having made a new friend. He thinks bluff means being naked."

"But if you take us down the rapids, you know we're going to impale ourselves on a rock, right?"

We approach the island, and the moment of decision is on us.

Left or right.

Right or left.

I look to Dyl, but his face gives nothing away. If I was searching the expression on his face for some kind of meaning, I'd simply think he needed a poop.

I look to my best friend. "He's changed the sign. I know he has."

So we make a decision.

We steer right.

We pass Dylan.

And as we do he smiles slyly, waving with the very tips of his fingers.

Oh no.

We paddle on, and as we turn a corner the placid, mirrorlike river disappears.

We appear to have steered into Niagara Falls.

We scream. Loudly. Wouldn't you?

22

I've never ridden the rapids before. Obviously.
The closest I got to it was when I was five and had
to share a bath with Dyl after a meal of beans on
toast.

And while that was distressing and scary, it's
nothing compared to this.

This is crazy stuff. There are waves bigger than
anything a surfer would dare tackle. And there are
bubbles. So many of them I reckon Dylan dropped
a bottle of dishwashing liquid in just to max the
fear factor. The rapids make it impossible to keep

your eyes open, especially when the kayak is writhing like a rodeo bull.

I try to row against the madness, thrusting my paddles in roughly, imagining the water's surface is Dyl's ugly mug, but it does nothing for our path or my anger.

Giraffles is doing his best too, his long arms clutching the paddles in the water, trying to steer us away from the rocks that jut out like mini icebergs.

We miss one to our left, then another, then a third, on our right this time, but as we straighten up we see another, like a shark's fin rushing toward us.

We scream and lean away, but we're going way too quick, which leaves us with only one option . . .

"Bail out!!"

I go first, but from the splash I hear, Giraffles doesn't need much persuading either.

Now, it may be spring, but nothing, NOTHING prepares us for the shock of the water as it blasts at our skin.

I kick to the surface and grab hold of the kayak. We can't lose it, and besides, I'm scared of where the next rock is coming from, so the boat is a handy shield.

"Grab on!" I yell at Giraffles, offering him the end of my paddle.

He hears me, and latches on. "Don't worry. I'll try to steer us toward the bank."

And he does—try, that is. But the only problem is that giraffes, like Giraffles, aren't known for their muscles. In fact, if they try to move quickly it often looks clumsy, like they only learned how to walk twenty minutes earlier, and as a result of this we remain at the mercy of the rapids, buffeted and rocked from wave to wave, grimacing at the foam that peppers our faces.

Finally, we start to move toward the bank, giving us the chance to pull ourselves back on board, but as soon as we sit back up, there are huge clumps of reeds and overhanging branches, at least thirty feet long, just waiting to gouge at us as we rush by.

"Brace yourself!" I yell, knowing it will be a lot easier for me to duck out of harm's way than my long-necked pal, but as we careen toward the bank, yet another obstacle appears, as three startled birds skitter from the undergrowth. Three birds, each with the brightest orange heads I have ever seen.

"The lesser spotted orange-crested warbler!" shouts Giraffles, and at that moment I'm so pleased he's my copilot and not Jonny, who would probably have been screaming "ELEPHANT!" by now.

It's still bad news though. Really bad. Geri was clear: Do NOT disturb their nesting area, at any cost, and here we were, plowing into it like a speedboat.

The reeds and branches envelop us, and all we can do is close our eyes, try and stay the right way up, and not kill any birds . . .

"You alive?" I ask as we come out the other side, eyes still closed. I don't dare look.

". . . Kind of!" says Giraffles, though he sounds . . . weird.

I allow my eyes to open, only to be hit by the most ridiculous of sights. Our kayak seems to have been transformed into some kind of bird sanctuary. From its tip to the cockpit, it is nest after nest after nest—and they're not empty either. Each of them is chock-full of orange-crested birds, adults, babies . . . there are even a few unhatched eggs teetering about as the waves continue to crash over us.

"What have we done?!" I scream. "If these nests fall overboard, we could wipe out the entire population. Geri will kill us!"

I look to Giraffles for the first time since emerging from the reeds, and at first I think he's put on some weird, elaborate hat, like the ones they used to wear on Easter in the olden days. Then I realize it's not a hat at all. It's a nest, and there are two angry-looking orange-crested warblers flying around his head, presumably convinced that Giraffles is trying to kidnap their babies. And what's worse, they seem to have spotted me too, as have their friends.

Next thing we know, we're inundated, batting them away from our faces as if they are a swarm of killer bees.

It's awful, it's terrible, I'm cold, I'm wet, and my butt still hurts. This is, without a doubt, the final-est of final straws, and it makes me shout a sentence I never thought I'd shout:

"GET ME OUT OF HERE!!!!!"

23

It's darker than dark when Giraffles and I get back to camp. So late that even the campfire has given up, smoking lazily instead of roaring a welcome.

There's also precious little of the feast left over for our hungry bellies, though from the piles of dirty dishes left for us to sort as part of our punishment, it's clear it was quite a meal. Thick, meaty stew and rice, by the looks of it, plus a sticky chocolate-coated banana, roasted in the fire before cream was stuck all over it. I'm so hungry that licking a few plates crosses my mind . . . Don't judge me.

Our afternoon wasn't quite so entertaining.

Geri flipped out when we arrived at the finish line disguised as a bird sanctuary.

"THERE WERE TWO RULES AND YOU BROKE THEM BOTH!" she roared. "No rapids, and no disturbing the nesting birds, so what happened, hhhhm?"

I tried to speak, but it turns out it was one of those rhetorical questions, when someone doesn't actually want an answer at all.

"Firstly, you could've killed yourself. Those rapids would challenge the strongest of explorers, never mind a couple of empty-headed fools like you, and secondly, we're only allowed to ride this river on the condition that we don't tamper with the delicate balance of nature. Didn't I tell you that the orange-crested warbler was in danger? Didn't I tell you that they were nesting and needed space? I did. So why, then, did you choose to camouflage your kayak not only with their nests, but with half of the population—AND more eggs than you'd find at an Easter parade?!"

I tried to speak again, but as Geri tried to catch her breath, it was Miss D. who butted in.

"So why did you both choose the rapids? Because I know you. I know you're not stupid."

"It was Dylan, Miss D."

"Not this again! I told you very clearly to steer clear of him. So why couldn't you do that? What did he do this time? Did he point you the wrong way? Or tamper with the sign?"

My brain stung with the desire to lie and scream, **"YES, BOTH OF THOSE THINGS!"** But I couldn't, could I? 'Cause it's not true, and 'cause, unlike Dyl, I have standards, which is a word he can't even spell, never mind understand. But I did have to stand my ground.

"He didn't exactly point us the wrong way, Miss D., but he's been messing with my head ever since we arrived. There was the nettles incident, then he strung me upside down from that tree. Honestly, Miss D., all he wants to do is ruin everything for me! He won't stop until he breaks me!"

I wanted to see Miss D. soften, not 'cause I was spinning her a line, but 'cause it was true and 'cause she knows what Dyl is like. She taught him too, back in the day.

But her pinched face didn't change a bit, and Geri's hardened like a sandwich left out in the sun.

"I'm sorry, boys, but any kind of provocation doesn't excuse what you did. We are lent this river on trust, and after today I'd be surprised if we're ever allowed to set foot here again. And as for your future on the rest of this trip, well, let's just say I've already checked train times home."

It felt like the world was ending in that second.

"You're . . . you're kicking us off the trip?" I asked.

Geri spoke up then. "I can't have recruits putting others at risk. Tomorrow is our final expedition, the most dangerous yet, and what happens if you decide to go rogue then, hhhm? How many lives would be at risk if you decide to ignore orders at sixty feet from the ground?"

184

"We'll do anything, Geri, Miss D., anything not to go home."

I looked at both of them, pleading with every muscle, every cell in my body. "I'll do cleanup for the rest of the trip, I'll even clean the toilet tent, with my tongue if I have to, I'll do anything as long as you don't send me home . . ."

"I think the cleaning up will be enough." Geri grimaced. "But first, the two of you will have to help me return all these nests to their rightful places. We can only hope that the eggs have not been damaged by your recklessness."

"We'll do anything, anything you say, and we're sorry."

I turned to Miss D., even though it wasn't my fault. "I really am." And I meant it, and we did it. We returned the nests, although hanging out on thin branches across the river felt just as dangerous as riding the rapids in the first place. But we did it with a smile and "Yes" and "Thank you" and plenty of "Anything you say."

Even now, when it's midnight and I ache from forehead to toe, and I'm still scrubbing pots in lukewarm water, I stay polite. And apologetic. So much so that at the end of the chores, when my eyes are closing, I hear Geri say the words I'm desperate to hear.

"Gentlemen, you have one more chance, but be warned: You are drinking in the LAST CHANCE SALOON. Don't mess this up, and don't let me down."

Relief floods my body. I'm too tired for elation, or even mild excitement.

Instead, I thank Geri and fall through the flaps into my tent.

I'm asleep before my head hits the pillow.

It's the last morning of our trip and we have a "big day ahead," though what that actually means none of us have a clue. Doesn't stop everyone from gossiping though.

"Am sure I saw four-wheelers parked over in the next field . . ."

"I reckon we'll be canyoning . . ."

"Segways!"

Jonny goes to open his mouth but is shut down before he declares he's seen Geri carrying an astronaut's helmet.

I don't mind what we do, to be honest. There's no way Geri's going to let us go home without a proper send-off, and I'm just relieved to still be here.

I give Dyl as much of a wide berth as I can, but I feel him looking at me and laughing, remembering how many times he's set me up, probably, and working out the next angle, the ultimate humiliation.

I milk the cow that he *isn't* holding in case he winds her up and she kicks me, and I do six loops around the toilet tent before stepping foot in it, just in case he's lurking, waiting to pull the whole thing down on top of me.

I'm not paranoid or anything—I'm just not taking any chances today. In fact, it's a relief when Geri calls us together, though I don't dare look her in the eye in case she takes it the wrong way and makes me ride Flossy to the train station.

"Recruits!" she barks, standing at attention. "By the end of the day, I will not be able to call you that anymore. By the end of the day you will have shed this skin. By the end of the day, you will be dirty and barely able to keep your eyes open. But you will be soldiers and warriors, each and every one of you."

It's a rallying call, that's for sure, and I think I can see Dyl getting emotional to my right. He probably reckons he'll be James Bond or something by nightfall.

"Your mission today is three-tiered," Geri continues. "It starts with a tough, one-hour ascent up a granite rock face that will not forgive any mistakes. It will hurt. Your muscles will ache; your fingers will feel like they no longer belong to you. But you must persevere, and waiting for you in the clouds is a treetop challenge that would test even the hoolock gibbons of eastern Bangladesh.

"You will be higher than any skyscraper in any city in the world, but you will have to navigate your way, branch to branch, before you can reach the final challenge: the single longest zip line this country has to offer. Clinging on for dear life you will hit speeds that would make a Formula One driver queasy. You will be traveling so fast the g-forces will blow your cheeks neatly behind your ears . . ."

I feel my cheeks clench with nerves . . . and not the ones on my face.

"Only when you feel your feet back on terra firma, and the dizziness turns into pure euphoria, will you be a Wild Out graduate. Many have failed, but that is not an option for any of you today. We go home triumphant, and we go home together!"

All right, so it's a bit dramatic—like she's been watching too many old videos of Winston Churchill's speeches from World War II—but it does the job, and we fall in behind her, marching to the mountain, carrying ropes so long that it looks like we'll be climbing all the way to Mars.

By the time we reach the bottom of the rock face, it actually feels like that might be the case. I can't describe how tall it is, because we can't even see the top. It creeps into a cloud that clings ominously to it.

"We've got to climb through the clouds?" Giraffles asks, though it'll only take five minutes for his neck to disappear into it.

"Into the unknown, Thomas, but the weather is fair . . . for now."

"For now?" I gulp.

"This valley has its very own climate. And the weather can turn in an instant. We will have to be at our very toughest, should it decide to test us."

I say nothing more, though my Adam's apple has swollen into a grapefruit. It dawns on me that I've never done this before. The others have— they had a full day of it while I was nursing my rashy rear—but for me, this is new territory. All right, I've climbed a few walls in my life, and fallen off way more than I'd like, but this is . . . different.

It's scary.

And it only gets scarier as I watch my friends spider their way up, struggling to get ahold of the mountain's rough face.

I wait, and I exhale, trying to hold my nerve, until my time comes, and Geri attaches a rope to my harness, and barks the order:

"Climb, Danny Mack. Climb."

25

Fifteen minutes in and I know three things:

1. I am tired.
2. I am not a mountain goat.
3. There's nothing more demoralizing than being outclimbed by a woman old enough to be a caveman's grandma.

I don't know where she gets her energy (or her robotic limbs) from, but I wouldn't mind a phone number so they could help me out too.

Everything hurts, from my fingers, which cling to the rock, to my arms (working muscles that I'm sure don't even exist), right down to my toes, which have to wedge themselves into crevices to stop me from falling backward.

"Use the power in your legs, Danny," Geri says. "They're stronger than your arms, so use them as levers to push you up."

I try, honestly I do, but I think all of Dyl's torture must've sapped me in some way. Removed my life force. I used to think I was a Jedi, and although I'm feeling greener than Yoda, that's definitely where the comparison ends.

I cling to the rock, craning my neck to

look above, and see everyone else practically skipping up. Giraffles is covering ten feet with every stretch of his arms, MandM are climbing side by side, arms and legs moving together so smoothly that they look like some kind of weird mutant spider. Lucky, I swear, is singing as he goes, and even Jonny seems to be nailing it just by not saying anything stupid for a while.

"I can do this," I say to myself. "If they can do it, then I can too." And I dig in, stretching my fingers to a good handhold, listening to Geri as she tells me again and again to "plot your path in advance. Like you're playing chess."

Chess? Right now I doubt I could win a game of tic-tac-toe, and this is proven by the fact that the piece of rock in my hand is even more tired than me and comes away from the mountain, leaving me to topple backward.

I make a noise that I have no idea how to spell, and grapple at the wall for some kind of safety, but it offers nothing and instead I fall, my stomach clenching, and my entire being screaming in fear.

I don't know how to describe how it feels to fall, except it's like I'm plummeting for minutes instead of seconds before the safety brake kicks in and I'm thrown into a hug with the rock, which doesn't offer much sympathy in return.

It hurts.

A lot.

Not that I see much in the way of sympathy from Geri either, although the others shout support from above.

"The clock is ticking, Mr. Mack," she says, and I see her frown doubly when she looks above.

"What is it?" I ask.

"Nothing," she replies, though her forehead says otherwise. "Keep moving, soldier. That's an order."

I know better than to ask any more questions and attach my grip back to the rock to start again, trying to remember everything she's already told me.

Progress is slow and painful, and now I don't

dare look up *or* down. It's too depressing to see my friends so far ahead, and too flippin' terrifying to see how far away the ground is. So instead, I focus on my hands above me, watching as the exertion turns my fingers blue.

"Come on!" I say through gritted teeth. "Don't let Dylan beat you."

And you know what? I find a rhythm. It might only be the rhythm of a watch whose battery is dying, but it's a rhythm all the same, and it's mine. Inch by inch, ledge by ledge, I edge slowly upward, and I feel my confidence grow. I start to feel almost a little bit proud, like I want my friends to see I'm catching up to them, so I look up, finally, ready to shout, but . . .

They've gone.

I can't see a single one of them, and I know they've not fallen because they would've taken me with them. Instead, they've been eaten by the cloud. Except it's not like any cloud I've ever seen before, and it's definitely not the light fluffy one that was casually hanging around when we set off.

This one is dark, and heavy, uglier even than Dylan. And the second I see it, I know what Geri had been staring at worriedly. You don't have to be a meteorologist to know what's lurking inside it, or the fact that it means trouble for us all.

"Er, Geri?" I offer.

"No time for chitchat, Danny. Keep climbing."

I don't say another word.

I have a feeling I'm going to need every breath in my lungs.

Do you ever wonder what it's like inside a cloud?

'Cause I do, and I'll tell you something: I never imagined it would be like this.

It's not light, or airy. There aren't birds relaxing on plump, cotton cloud-pillows, snacking on worms and singing to one other.

It's dark and damp, and it's hard to even see where your fingers are, never mind whether they're attached to the rock that'll stop you from falling. The air is cold. It clings to my face and hands, but there's no way of warming up my fingers or any other part of me. Apart from by climbing. The faster I climb, the speedier the blood flows, and the warmer I'll get.

I don't need Geri to tell me this either. I'm smart enough to do the math, no matter what my brother might tell you.

So I double my efforts—triple them, even. Put every bit of muscle that I have into it, no matter how much it hurts.

And I go up, up, up.

Then, from somewhere above, sweet music. Not the birds chirping, but a Giraffles shouting.

"Danny? Danny, bro, is that you?"

I squint through the cloud, dampness hugging my face.

"Yeah! Where are you?"

"Straight up, see? Here. At the top!"

I squint, but it's really thick now, like in one of those films where a cloud swallows everyone alive. Except when you're watching the film, you know it's fake and your mouth's full of popcorn. All I can taste at the moment is fear, and it's neither sweet nor salted.

"Keep looking," he yells. "I can see you. Just barely. And keep going. You're nearly there!'"

That's all I need to hear to propel me on, and I power up, even shocking Geri, who doesn't look as in control as she usually does. In fact, for the first time since we've met her, she looks her age, which at the moment seems to be pushing 172.

"Here," says Giraffles, no longer needing to shout. "Reach up . . ." and I do, feeling two hands hoist me roughly over the rocks, not that I feel it—there's too much adrenaline coursing through my body. It's just a relief to know that I'm not going to die on that mountain's face, though, judging by the expressions of the others huddled around me, we might be about to freeze to death while sitting at the top.

"How long have you been waiting?" I ask Giraffles.

"Not long, really. Soon as the cloud dropped,

everyone slowed down. Can't believe how cold it is; it's not even freaking winter."

"No one ever said it would be easy!" booms Geri behind us, slicing through the cloud like an elderly robotic ninja. "This is the life of a soldier. Now sit together. Huddle close and preserve heat. Eat, refuel, then we move on."

"Er, Geri . . . ?" asks Jonny, and we wait for his latest piece of brilliance. "Shouldn't we, you know, go back down? The weather's a bit . . . scary, isn't it?"

Mouths open, jaws drop. I swear that somewhere in the distance I hear an angel sing "HALLELUJAH!" because, you know what, Jonny's speaking something resembling sense, isn't he? It's dark, it's cold, and it's foggy, so calling it quits and heading down to safety and a steaming mug of hot chocolate makes sense to a lot of us. MandM have already stood up and are attaching themselves back onto the ropes.

Geri, however, has other ideas.

"Down? Down?! There is no down. Well, there is, but we can't go down the way we came up. Because none of you know how to rappel, do you?"

Heads shake. A lot of us don't even know what the word means . . .

"Can't we get a helicopter to collect us?" asks Lucky, whose dad probably has a couple tucked away in the garage.

"Or an eagle with a saddle," adds Jonny helpfully, which makes Geri even more determined to push on.

"If we move quickly and with togetherness, we will be fine. This weather wasn't in the forecast, so I'm sure it will clear quickly. Trust me."

And we do. Of course we do. 'Cause, to be honest, there isn't another choice . . .

For fifteen minutes, we stumble along the rock face, hoods up and mouths closed. It's slippery underfoot, like someone's poured liquid soap under our shoes, and there's the constant echo of shouts as, one after another, children fall flat on their butts.

"GET UP!" yells Geri, every time. **"GET UP, AND GET ON!"**

But that's easier said than done, because the weather decides that instead of clearing up as she predicted, it's going to dig its heels in and stick its tongue out in the worst way imaginable.

It starts with a huge rasping raspberry of a wind that comes from nowhere, battering our faces and whipping at our raincoats.

"It's OK," shouts Geri, "this is good! The wind will blow the clouds away quicker. The sun will be out in no time."

But the weather is obviously listening and—oh boy—it does not like Geri, because it reaches into its huge bag of tricks and throws a belter of a weapon straight into her face.

Rain.

And not just the pitter-patter variety.

No, this is rain that has been sharpened

into tiny, lethal arrowheads and spat, by the thousands, directly into our faces, forcing us to hunch over to protect our eyes, while struggling with the treacherously slippery rock beneath our feet.

"Move quickly but carefully. The woods are only two hundred yards ahead!" Geri squeals, barely loud enough to beat the sounds of our complaints.

But the woods might as well be two hundred miles away, 'cause the weather hurls the double whammy of rain AND wind at us, and it's a murderous act with disastrous results.

Many of us are on the small side, and as a result don't weigh an awful lot. Jonny in particular would barely trouble a set of scales, but he's not the one most affected by the gusts hammering us.

Geri is.

I see it first, but can barely believe my eyes . . .

"Giraffles, oh boy, look! This isn't good . . ."

"What is it?" he replies, not wanting to raise his face to the daggery rain.

"The wind. It's lifting her. It's lifting her up . . . off her feet!"

And it is, I swear it is. I don't know how, 'cause after all, Geri is part cyborg, and surely cyborg skeletons weigh more than human ones, no matter how old.

But obviously they don't, because no matter how hard she tries, Geri is repeatedly plucked momentarily from her feet, before being dropped to the ground.

There is a yell. A yell of pain. But it doesn't last long, as Geri's pain seems to turn to fear. The slippery rocks start to tilt away from her like a slide, and with the rain and the wind still swirling, she moves away from us, quicker and quicker.

Away from us, and closer and closer to the edge of the mountain that we've just climbed.

"Miss D.!" Giraffles and I squeal as one, but

Miss D. is bringing up the rear and too far back to do a thing.

All we can do is watch through our hands as our leader and guide hurtles, quite literally, toward the abyss . . .

27

Time does not stand still, or slow down.

Not even close.

Everything speeds up, especially Geri, her thin bones skidding over the rock like she's riding a bobsled.

We watch as she grapples for something to hang on to, anything that would take the edge off the pace she's motoring at.

Tree roots offer a bit of help, but no matter how strong her robotic hands are, they aren't tough enough to hang on for longer than a few seconds, and she's left to ricochet on, powerless.

"MISS D.!" MandM yell, their two voices definitely better than one. But although Miss D. has no problem hearing them, there is no way she can reach Geri in time to be any kind of help.

Dyl neither: He's too busy trying to look like the weather isn't troubling him to realize it's troubling him too much to help.

And this is when something surprising happens. Giraffles sticks his neck out. Quite literally.

Now, Giraffles is brilliant, and that's why he's my best friend, but he's not exactly known for his bravery. He'd run a mile if a spider spun a web within a hundred yards of him. But when he sees Geri flailing past us, something comes over him, and those epically long legs of his ignore the wind and take off after her.

For the first few strides it looks completely pointless and weird, frankly, but that doesn't get in the way of him trying—and you know what, the gap starts to close.

"GERI!" he shouts. **"THERE'S A BOULDER! GRAB IT! PLEASE!"**

I see what he's shouting about, and there's every chance Geri will be able to do it. In fact, she has to, 'cause beyond that there's nothing else to grab except air. And although there's plenty of that between the cliff edge and the valley below, it's not going to be any help whatsoever.

Geri knows that too, she's a warrior after all, and so she digs deep, arms outstretched as the rock zooms closer.

Giraffles, meanwhile, is still running along, or at least he was, because as Geri's fingers manage to make contact with the boulder, he flings himself headfirst onto the ground, sliding like a soccer player after scoring from the halfway line.

I'm still rooted to the spot in fear when I hear Giraffles shouting at me over his shoulder.

"Danny, get the others. You need to grab my legs, and don't you dare let go!"

It's not a plea we can ignore, and we belt after him, fast enough to reach his ankles without throwing ourselves into the abyss as well.

Giraffles is still on his belly, head pointing down to the cliff's edge, arms stretching out for what looks like an infinity, in the direction of Geri, whose grip is loosening by the second. He glances back over his shoulder at us. **"HOLD ON TIGHT,"** he says. **"AND WHEN I SAY** *PULL,* **PULL!"**

With that, his attention flies back to our leader, and he barks instructions just like she has for the past three days. It'd be really impressive if it wasn't so ridiculously scary, scary enough for Geri to do exactly what he asks, grabbing on to his hands with her own.

"PULL, DANNY, PULL!"

I don't need telling again, and nor do the others.

We yank at Giraffles' elastic legs, digging our heels into the skiddy rock to stop ourselves from toppling over.

Others join in, grabbing us from behind and pulling too, until it feels like we're the rope in an enormous tug-of-war, so goodness knows how poor Giraffles must feel.

He doesn't moan though, or if he does we can't hear him because his head is still facedown in the dirt. But we feel him slide closer and closer to us, and see Geri following close behind.

"Don't stop! Don't stop," screams Miss D. as she gingerly steps beside us, grabbing onto Geri's elbows as they slide into range.

We do what she tells us, and with one final tug, we all fall backward into a pile, Geri catapulting to the top of the mound, safe, but in pain, offering two words that none of us really want to hear.

"It's broken."

I hope she's not badly hurt, I really do, but I also hope she's referring to a small part of her body, rather than our way back down to safety . . .

28

"You all right there, Geri?" I ask, as we head as speedily as we can for the forest.

"Like I'm sitting on the comfiest recliner in the world," she answers with a grimace and a dollop of sarcasm.

I can't blame her. Last place I'd want to be when I'm nearly two hundred years old and have a smashed-up ankle is on my idiot brother's back, especially when he's reveling in the glory of being the savior. Honestly, I thought he was going to do a hundred push-ups before lifting her for the first time, just to get his guns pumping and primed.

I rolled my eyes but said nothing. I wasn't going to give him any ammo after what he'd done to me over the last few days.

"Keep going, recruits," Geri rallies. "As soon as we hit the trees the weather won't be half as bad."

"It couldn't get any worse, could it?" asks Lucky, his trademark smile missing from his face. He does have a point though: The tiny arrowhead raindrops have been replaced by a billion massive, bucket-sized ones, the type where a single drop would soak every inch of you more effectively than a waterfall.

Still, it drives us on, and finally, finally, we feel the trees take the brunt of the clouds instead of our heads.

"Well done, everyone!" beams Miss D., but the smile on her face looks more like relief than joy. "Not far now."

We know, though, that that is not exactly true. There's still the walkways in the trees to pass, and then the zip line—and how on earth are we going to get Geri through all that, 'cause although Dyl thinks he's strong, even he can't do it.

It's too much—even just the thought of it—there has to be another way. I pull my phone out of my pocket and stare at the screen.

No bars whatsoever.

"Anyone got a signal so we can ring Mountain Rescue?"

Hands reach into soaked pockets and phones appear, some better than others but none of them managing to reach a satellite successfully, not even Lucky's, which is so high-tech it should be able to morph into a helicopter and fly us down.

But just as our spirits sink once more, a lone voice cuts through the gloom.

"IT'S WORKING!" Jonny shrieks. **"IT'S FINALLY WORKING!"**

I resist the temptation to shout *What, your brain? Finally!* because he's looking at his phone, the screen lighting his delighted face.

"I've got a signal. Four bars. Count 'em, count 'em!" and he starts doing a little jig, which almost turns into a full-on break-dance, and ends up with the phone slipping out of his fingers and onto the stony ground.

It bounces in slow motion, every one of us yelling, **"NOOOOOOOOOOOOO"** as one.

Our hearts refuse to beat as he snatches it up, desperate to assess the damage.

"It's OK, it's OK—it's not smashed, it's not smashed."

"Just call the cops, will you, Jonny?" Lucky demands. "Please!"

So Jonny bashes in nine-one-one, puts the phone on speaker, and then we hear the greatest words we have ever heard:

"Nine-one-one."

YES!!!

"What is your emergen—"

Then . . . nothing. Silence. And nothing on the screen either. The blue hue flicks to black, and it hangs limply in Jonny's hand, exhausted. Dead.

"My battery died!" he says like his world has been snatched from him.

"Maybe if you weren't checking it every minute then you'd still have some juice left," Lucky shouts.

"It's not my fault. At least my phone got a signal before it died. Yours is worthless!"

It goes on like this for a couple of minutes, the disappointment turning into frustration and then full-on anger.

But I don't join in. There's no point. Instead, I turn up the collar of my coat and walk on.

"Where you going, Danny?" Giraffles asks.

"Down. Home. Hopefully."

He nods and walks after me, and soon the others start to follow too.

29

I have always loved watching monkeys. Gibbons especially.

Not that I've ever actually seen one, obviously. We do have exotic breeds of vermin back in the city—rats, mostly—but not much in the way of monkeys.

I've seen plenty of them on TV, though. Seen how effortless they make it look, traversing from tree to tree, never pausing or thinking for a second that they might fall to their death.

But it's only now I realize how inferior we

humans are—'cause we aren't swinging from anything to anything. All we're trying to do is walk across slightly slippery wooden walkways. And we're even doing that badly.

We aren't even in Madagascar, we're just in the middle of nowhere, though we are completely soaked and utterly, utterly annoyed.

We've been making our way through the trees for over an hour now, and to be fair, it's partly taking so long 'cause the planks under our feet are completely soaked, and they've collected all the muck off the rained-on leaves, which is making it feel like an ice rink.

On top of that, we have to keep stopping because there are obviously no bathrooms at the top of trees—or bushes either—and nobody ever needs to pee at the same time.

Oh, and our team leader has a smashed-up leg and needs carrying.

To be honest, it's a wonder we've managed to move at all.

But then a voice comes from the gloom.

"Well done, troops. You've almost made it. Look ahead and you'll see one last rope bridge for us to cross, before the final zip line down."

We squint into the darkness. And it really is dark, despite it only being midafternoon. The trees are thick and dense, like something from the Amazon, and we can tell from the rain still puncturing through that the clouds are no better up above. If anything, it must be raining even harder.

"Can you see it?" Giraffles asks. "The bridge?"

"Yeah, up there. And to the right a bit." Though to call it a bridge may be a stretch. Bridges are usually designed by engineers, aren't they? Who go to college for half a lifetime before they're trusted to make anything. This looks like it was designed by a seven-year-old in science class, then knocked together during a couple of wet lunchtimes.

It's long, probably ninety feet or so across, with a big old dip in the middle, like an elephant's been napping there for the past eighteen months. My confidence in it doesn't grow as we move closer either. I can see that rungs are missing along it, and that the rope is fraying and straining in places, as if the storm has left it exhausted.

"It may look rickety, but trust me," says Geri. "This bridge has stood for years, and it'll stand for many more." But there's that look on her face again, the one she was wearing when she first saw the cloud falling over the mountain.

"This is how it works," she continues. "We cross the bridge in groups of three, because space on the zip-line platform is small. One by one, you will travel down the zip line, and the waiting passengers must crank the pulley back up to the top in preparation for the next child. Got it?"

We nod and she smiles. "I know this has been difficult—a challenge, even. But you have handled it admirably and I promise you, the drama is over. Finished. Done."

Which is exactly when the thunder rumbles, scaring us half to death.

Maybe it's the weather gods laughing at Geri or maybe we are, actually, doomed, but the storm doesn't hesitate. It tells us it means

business: There's no rumbling in the distance; the thunder is on top of us already and the rain follows angrily, puncturing the last of the tree line and hammering on the rope bridge, making it shake with impact.

"Let's GO!" shouts Miss D., who I reckon will now swear off school trips for the rest of her life, and we shuffle on, the slap of the rain on our shoulders and heads making us flinch.

Up close, the bridge looks no safer than it did from a distance; in fact, it looks terrifying. But I keep the sight of the zip line in my mind. One more ride, I tell myself, one more ride and we'll be back on the ground. It looks like the others agree, because there's no shortage of volunteers to go first, no matter how shaky the bridge seems.

After much persuasion from Miss D., Geri goes with the first two, shuffling across the wooden planks like she's done it a million times before, though I see the grimace on her face with every movement, the bridge creaking and buckling as she goes.

It seems to take an age for the first three to get over, and Geri almost needs pushing down the zip line, not wanting to leave anyone behind. Passage across the gorge is slow, and while the zip line looks super speedy on the way down, winding the pulley system back up takes time and energy. All we can do as we wait is try and keep warm, though it's impossible to stay dry as the rain falls with greater and greater venom.

Minutes pass and the weather worsens—even the wind has picked up as well, presumably because it felt left out.

But we can't let it stop us, and slowly but surely there are fewer and fewer of us waiting on the wrong side of the bridge. In fact, there's only five left: me, MandM, Miss D., and Dyl, of course.

"OK, Dylan," says Miss D., "you take Marcus and Maureen, and Danny and I will follow last."

But Dyl, in true annoying style, has to have the last word. "I'll wait with our Danny, Miss D. With my training it makes sense for me to go last. I can firefight anything that comes my way, no problem."

Honestly, the boy is so cocky. If he shoved his chest out any farther he'd be pushing us off the platform and into the void.

"Are you OK with that, Danny?" she asks, and I nod, 'cause I am. What else is Dyl going to do, push me to my death? Can't see how he'd explain that one away to Mom.

So, with one final look over her shoulder, Miss D. shepherds MandM across to the far platform, though how she manages to get them down the zip line one at a time, I have no idea.

Five minutes later, and once her terrified tones die away as the zip line whooshes to the ground, there's just the two of us left. Me and Dyl. Beauty and the Beast.

"Well, then, little brother," he beckons, "shall we?"

And there's nothing else to say, except yes.

Except I don't get to say it, do I?

'Cause that is the moment when the lightning strikes.

30

The noise is sickening, like the tree is screaming in pain as the lightning cuts it in two.

It splits slowly at first, but gets quicker as the tear gets deeper, and I realize quickly that although the tree was some distance from us, it would definitely crush us on its way down.

"DYLAN," I yell, all rivalry forgotten, **"JUMP! NOW!"**

But all he does, the airhead that he is, is turn and look directly at it, eyes widening as it begins to plummet toward him. He's frozen. Rigid. And for the first time in my life, I see he's terrified.

"Dyl! JU—"

But there isn't time, and without thinking I jump straight at him, tackling him around the waist. I feel his legs give, and my momentum throws us sideways as I feel the rush of wind and vibrations of tree on earth. It's like an echo. People probably feel it all the way down in Australia.

As soon as the shaking stops, Dyl throws me aside with an embarrassed huff.

"Get off me, weirdo!"

"Oh, I'm sorry, for a second there I thought I was saving your stupid life. Remind me to forget next time."

But I don't think he can hear me, as his eyes land on the fallen tree and we both see just how HUGE it is.

"Is that a redwood? I've seen them on TV . . ."

"It's massive, that's what it is."

And we both realize, I think, just how close we were to being squashed flat by it. It. Is.

MAMMOTH. Cut it up and light it and you could warm a town for a good couple of years, not that we had any intention of breaking out a hacksaw.

All I want is to get back down to earth and get out of here.

But as I pull myself on top of the trunk, I see the worst thing imaginable. The tree has fallen across the gorge, and has completely trashed the rope bridge. There's not a plank or even a frayed rope to be seen.

There's a fresh crack of thunder and an immediate flash of lightning that lights our faces, and no matter how hard he tries to hide it, I know that Dyl is just as scared as I am. In fact, he seems more scared, 'cause his ability to think straight is gone.

"What are we going to do now?" he asks, and he looks younger, like a little kid who's just dropped his lunch money down the drain. I think he might be about to cry.

I know I could tell him to grow up, or ask him

what his ROTC training would tell him to do, but I also realize in that instant that there's only one person who's going to get us down off this mountain, and it's not G.I. Joe whimpering over there. It's me.

So I look closer at the fallen tree. It's even bigger than I first thought. Maybe, just maybe, it might have bridged the entire chasm itself, and if we're really careful we can just walk across it to the other side.

But no, that would be way too easy, wouldn't it? Because of the way that it's fallen, there's still a real gap between it and the zip-line platform. What I don't know yet is whether we can jump the final bit.

I explain to Dyl that we need to find out, that one of us needs to shimmy along it to work out how far that jump would be; but when he pulls his soaked head so far inside his coat that he looks like a terrified turtle, I realize that person is me.

So off I go, to the edge of the void, where the

rope bridge used to begin, and sit on the tree trunk, a leg on either side. What follows is clumsy and embarrassing, as I scoot along the bark, like a dog trying to scratch an itchy butt.

The movements are small, but the trunk is solid. I manage to make progress without dislodging the tree or sending myself hurtling into the abyss.

Within minutes, which feel like hours, I'm far enough along to be able to see clearly, and I decide:

1. The gap is jumpable.
2. The gap would be the biggest jump of my life.
3. Standing on the tree could make it capsize and send both of us to our deaths.

It's not ideal, and the thunderstorm continues to spit rainy daggers in my direction. How long until lightning strikes another tree, which wipes out our tree and makes it absolutely impossible to get across?

There are too many things to worry about.

I shimmy backward (this should be an Olympic

sport), until I find myself face-to-face with Dyl again.

"It's good news," I lie, leaving out my concerns about the tree toppling into the abyss. "There's a gap at the other end, but it's jumpable, especially for you."

That's not a lie, 'cause he's way bigger than me, and he's been jumping for years now (even if that is mostly on me).

He obviously isn't keen on the idea, but at the same time I can see he doesn't want to look scared in front of me, so after a bit of stalling he begins to shuffle across, which lacks the technique I've developed, but I see him reach the end of the tree in record time.

I watch from the bank, not daring to step on the tree in case the weight of us both is too much. The tension eats at me, as does the wind and the rain and the constant threat of being deep-fried by a lightning bolt, and for a while I wonder if Dyl is going to jump at all, or whether the fear has totally grabbed him.

But then, just as I'm about to shout, he jumps, and I watch as the tree wobbles beneath him. For one horrible second I think momentum is going to make it tumble down, leaving me stranded. I even consider grabbing it and trying to hold it steady until I realize the weight of it could easily catapult me to my doom.

By the time I've made all these realizations, I see that Dylan has landed, safe and cocky, on the other side, and is already winching up the zip line. He probably won't even wait for me, because why break the habit of a lifetime now?

As another rumble hits above me, I sit astride the trunk and shuffle my way along. The bark is wet and slippery, and I feel my hands slide off it on several occasions, testing my balance and my nerve.

I'm fighting off rain, wind, and a dollop of low clouds, just to really test me, and it doesn't help when the tree trunk starts to groan and ache, reminding me that it is in no way happy about holding me like this. I ignore it and shuffle on, right to the very end.

The gap seems bigger than it did five minutes ago—ten times bigger—and suddenly I'm no longer sitting on a log but standing on a brick wall, back in the city, and there are little kids laughing and pointing at me, and I don't know if I can do this anymore. I don't want to stand up. But I don't want to stay here either, especially since Dyl has hauled the zip line handle up to the top and is already fastening his safety line to it.

And you know what? By doing this, he does me the biggest favor, and I stand up instantly. I want him to see me make this jump, to see that no matter how many nettles rub against my butt, or how many times he traps me thirty feet in the air, he can't beat me. 'Cause I'm Danny Mack, and without me, his sad little life would've been squashed flat minutes ago.

But just as I make a crazy note to remind him of this every five minutes for the rest of our lives, there's an explosion from above. A crack of thunder, the loudest yet, and with it a blinding forked flash that zigzags behind me, hitting the exposed roots of the tree on which I'm standing. The trunk trembles with the impact, and there's a new noise, a sizzle, and I don't need to look over my shoulder to know that the tree is on fire.

"YOU'RE KIDDING ME!" I wail, because how can anything as wet as this tree still be catching fire? But from the smell, I know it's doing its very best.

So I do the only thing I can do: I look forward, not at the gap between me and safety, but at the lip that I need to land on. I can do this, I tell myself. I'm a free runner, I'm an explorer, I'm a soldi—

And then the tree starts to give way beneath me.

I feel it tip and turn and know that the moment is now—I need to go, throw myself forward before the spinning log sucks me down into the gorge.

With every muscle and every sinew bursting, I launch myself, eyes fixed on the ledge. Wind whips my face and rain stabs at my eyes, but I ignore it. I've done too much these last few days, and had too many things done to me, to fail now, and with each inch I cover, I feel my confidence grow.

"ARGHHHHHH!" I yell, arms outstretched and braced, but the momentum seems to stop, and that forward motion morphs into a downward one. The ledge seems to be farther instead of nearer, and I hear the tree trunk give up its fight as it topples headfirst into the gorge.

I feel pain rip at my fingers as they bite into the stony ledge. The rest of my body slams into the ridge below, bruising me instantly, but my fingers hold on.

I can do this, I tell myself, not even considering for a second about shouting for Dyl— he's probably zipping down the line by now anyway. I dig my toes into the wall, finding a crevice I can use as leverage.

I push, my legs straightening, my fingers on fire, until I can wedge my elbows onto the ledge instead. The wind gusts at me and pulls at my pant legs, but I'm too close now to let it win, and with one final, monumental effort I swing my left leg up and onto the ledge, my body rolling with it, to safety.

Everything hurts—my hands, my ribs, my legs, my brain—but all I can do is laugh. I turn my head up to the clouds and I laugh myself silly, drinking the rain as I do so.

"You," Dyl sneers, "are a maniac. And don't even think about telling the others that you saved me up here. 'Cause let's face it, no one will believe you."

Tucking his legs up and clinging to the zip line, he begins his final, speedy descent, leaving me alone, at the top, laughing like a lunatic and feeling like the king of the world.

31

We wave at Geri from the window of the bus, and she salutes back, perfectly balanced despite the cast-iron skillet tied to her ankle and the crutches wedged under her arm.

It wasn't an emotional goodbye—elderly cyborg warriors don't tend to cry often, probably 'cause it damages their wiring. The salute and the smile said all she needed to say.

Miss D. doesn't say a lot either. She just shakes her head endlessly while whispering something about "never again." Looks like she could use a hug, to be honest.

There's plenty of chatter on the bus though. Everyone's got a story to tell, some of them true, a lot of them way overexaggerated. Everyone wants to be a hero, I suppose.

Me? Not so much. I haven't told anyone about what happened at the top of the mountain. Not because of what Dyl said—I don't care if people believe him over me. I know what happened and so does he, and we'll carry that over the next few days and weeks and months.

I am watching Dyl though, sitting a few rows ahead. On his own, of course.

And I'm watching him for a very good reason. Before we got on the bus, we had to make ourselves a packed lunch. And I managed to do a good thing. Well, for me at least.

I got my old friend Giraffles to distract Dylan, while I put on some gloves and swapped the lettuce in his sandwich for something equally green, but way more spicy.

I've never eaten nettles, but I hear they carry quite a kick. It might be a while before he gets hungry, but that's OK. I can wait.

I turn my head and look out the window as the landscape rolls past.

There are fields and mountains and electrical towers as big as iron giants, and in the distance, there's a big old beast, grazing on some grass.

I look at Giraffles and MandM and Lucky and poor old Jonny, and we point, and smile, and say, all at the same time . . .

"LOOK! A RHINO!"

And then we laugh so hard we think we'll never laugh again.

Until, that is, our Dylan opens up his lunch box . . .

ACKNOWLEDGMENTS

Huge thanks to Jodie, Emily, Philippa, Robin, Pete, Sam, Rachel, Beth, and definitely Fiz, who edited on the dash without ever breaking sweat!
—Andy & Phil

Big love to Albie, Elsie, Stanley, Louise (xx), Rufus, Bebe, and Nancy. You lot make me proper happy.
—Phil